PUSHI

THE SPECTRE
OF
ALEXANDER
WOLF

'A work of great potency'
GUARDIAN

'A weird meditation on death, war and sex'
PARIS REVIEW

'A finely wrought novel, tense and enigmatic'
TIMES LITERARY SUPPLEMENT

GAITO GAZDANOV (1903–1971) joined the White Army aged just sixteen and fought in the Russian Civil War. Exiled in Paris from the 1920s onwards, he eventually became a nocturnal taxi-driver and quickly gained prominence on the literary scene as a novelist, essayist, critic and short-story writer, and was greatly acclaimed by Maxim Gorky, among others.

BRYAN KARETNYK is a British writer and translator. His translations for Pushkin Press include several works by Gaito Gazdanov, Irina Odoevtseva and Rynunosuke Akutagawa. He is also the editor of the Penguin Classics anthology *Russian Émigré Short Stories from Bunin to Yanovsky*.

THE SPECTRE OF ALEXANDER WOLF

GAITO GAZDANOV

TRANSLATED FROM THE RUSSIAN
BY BRYAN KARETNYK

PUSHKIN PRESS CLASSICS

Pushkin Press
Somerset House, Strand
London WC2R 1LA

The Spectre of Alexander Wolf was originally published in
1947–48 as *Prizrak Aleksandra Vol'fa* in the Russian-language
journal *Novyi Zhurnal* (The New Review), New York.

First published by Pushkin Press in 2013
This edition published 2023

1 3 5 7 9 8 6 4 2

ISBN 13: 978-1-80533-023-3

Designed and typeset by Tetragon, London
Printed and bound in the United Kingdom by Clays Ltd, Elcograf S.p.A.

www.pushkinpress.com

THE SPECTRE
OF
ALEXANDER
WOLF

O F ALL MY MEMORIES, of all my life's innumerable sensations, the most onerous was that of the single murder I had committed. Ever since the moment it happened, I cannot remember one day passing when I haven't regretted it. No punishment for it ever threatened me, because it occurred in the most exceptional of circumstances and it was clear that I couldn't have acted otherwise. Moreover, no one other than I knew about it. It was one of those countless episodes of the Civil War; in the general course of contemporary events it could be looked upon as an insignificant detail, all the more so as during those few minutes and seconds prior to the incident its outcome concerned only the two of us—myself and another man, unknown to me. Then I was alone. No one else had any part in this.

I couldn't faithfully describe what led up to the event because everything was such a blur, a mark of almost all fighting in any war, the participants of which least of all conceive of what's happening in reality. It was summer, in southern Russia, and we were on our fourth day of continuous, disorderly troop manoeuvres, to an accompaniment of gunfire and sporadic fighting. I'd completely lost all concept of time; I couldn't even say where I was exactly. I remember only the sensations, which could just as easily have been elicited in other circumstances—the feeling of hunger, thirst, terrible fatigue; I hadn't slept these past two and a half nights. There was a torrid heat, and the air hung with the faint smell of smoke; an hour previously we'd made our way out of a forest, which was ablaze on one side, and there, where the sunlight couldn't penetrate, a great straw-coloured shadow slowly pressed forward. I was so desperate for sleep; I remember thinking at the time that it would have been utter bliss to stop, lie down on the scorched grass and drop off, forgetting about everything. However, this was the one thing that I couldn't do, and so I continued through the hot, drowsy haze, swallowing my saliva and periodically rubbing my eyes, which were irritated by the heat and a lack of sleep.

I recall that when we were passing through a small grove, I leant against a tree and, standing for what I thought to be only a second, I drifted off with the long-familiar sound of gunfire in the background. When I opened my eyes there was no one around. I cut across the grove and set out on the road, in the direction I thought my comrades to have taken. Almost immediately I was outstripped by a Cossack astride a swift bay horse; he waved to me and shouted something I couldn't make out. After some time, I had the good fortune to come across a scraggy black mare whose rider obviously had been killed. She was bridled and had a Cossack saddle on her back, and she was nibbling at the grass, constantly swishing her long, wiry tail. As soon as I mounted her, she set off at a gallop.

I rode along a deserted, winding road; every now and then the occasional little grove would obscure a bend in the track. The sun stood high in the sky, and the air almost hummed from the heat. Although I was riding quickly, I still have a false impression of everything happening in slow motion. I was still desperate for sleep; this longing filled my body and my consciousness, and because of it everything seemed lingering and drawn out, although in fact, of course, it couldn't have been so. The fighting had ceased; all was quiet. I saw no one either behind or ahead of me. Suddenly, at one of the turns veering off almost at a right angle, my horse fell hard, at full tilt. I went tumbling down with her, landing on a soft, dark—because I closed my eyes—patch, but managed to free my leg from the stirrup and escaped almost unharmed by the fall. The bullet had hit her right ear and passed straight through her head. Getting to my feet, I turned around and saw, not very far off, coming towards me at what seemed a slow, heavy gallop, a rider astride a great white horse. I recall that my rifle had been missing for quite some time; I'd most probably left it in the grove where I fell asleep. I still had a revolver, though, and with some difficulty managed to pull it out of its tight, new holster. I stood for a few seconds, holding the revolver in my hand; it was so quiet that I could distinctly make out the dry sobbing of hooves against the cracked earth, the horse's heavy breathing, and another sound, similar to the rapid jingling of a little bunch of metallic rings. I saw the rider let go of the reins and shoulder his rifle, which, until that point, he had been carrying atilt. It was then that I fired. He jerked up in his saddle, slumped down and fell slowly to the ground. I stood motionless next to the body of my horse

11

for two or three minutes. Still I wanted to sleep, and that same agonizing weariness persisted. I managed, however, to consider the fact that I had no idea what lay ahead of me or whether I would even be alive for much longer, but the irrepressible urge to see just whom I'd killed compelled me to stir from my spot and approach him. No other distance, anywhere and at any time, has been as difficult for me to traverse as those fifty or sixty metres that separated me from the fallen rider; nevertheless, I walked towards him, dragging my feet over the hot, cracked earth. Finally I reached him. He was a man of around twenty-two or twenty-three; his cap had blown off to one side, and his head, fair-haired, lay at an awkward angle on the dusty road. He was rather handsome. I leant over him and saw that he was dying; bubbles of pink foam frothed up and burst on his lips. He opened his dull eyes, said nothing, and closed them again. I stood over him and looked into his face, still clutching the now superfluous revolver with my numbing fingers. Suddenly, a light gust of warm air carried to me the scarcely audible clatter of horses' hooves, and then I remembered the danger I could yet face. The dying man's white horse, pricking up its ears in alarm, stood only a few paces away from him. It was a great stallion, very well groomed and clean, its back a little dark with sweat. Of particular note were the horse's exceptional speed and endurance; I sold it a few days before I fled Russia, to a German settler who supplied me with an enormous quantity of provisions and paid me a vast sum of worthless money. The revolver I used to take the shot—it was a wonderful Parabellum—I cast into the sea, and from all this I was left with nothing more than a painful memory that haunted me everywhere Fate took me. However, the memory grew dimmer by and by, and with time it almost shed that initial feeling of constant, burning regret. But I was never able to forget it entirely. Many a time, whether it be summer or winter, by the sea or deep within the continent of Europe, I, mind empty, would close my eyes, and suddenly from the depths of memory that sultry day in southern Russia would draw once more into focus, and then those same feelings would re-emerge with all their former intensity. I saw again the enormous rose-grey shadow of the forest fire and its gradual progression amidst the crackle of burning twigs and branches; I felt that unforgettable, agonizing weariness and the almost overwhelming desire to sleep, the merciless brilliance of the sun, the ringing heat, and finally the mute recollection of the revolver's weight in my grasp, its rough grip as if for ever imprinted on my skin, the slight swaying of the black foresight in front of my right eye—and then the fair-haired head on the grey, dusty road, and the face, transformed by the approach of death, that very death that I, only a second ago, had summoned out of the untold future.

I was sixteen years old when all this took place, and, as such, this murder marked the beginning of my independence; I'm not even certain that it hasn't left an unconscious mark on everything I was destined to learn and see thereafter. In any case, the circumstances accompanying it and everything in its connection all came to the fore with particular clarity many years later, in Paris. It transpired because I fell into the possession of a collection of short stories by an English author, whose name I had never before heard. The book was entitled *I'll Come Tomorrow*, after the first story in the collection. There were three stories in all: "I'll Come Tomorrow", "The Goldfish" and "The Adventure in the Steppe". They were exceptionally well written, and of particular excellence were the narrative's taut, flawless rhythm and the author's distinctive manner of seeing things in quite an original light. However, neither "I'll Come Tomorrow" nor "The Goldfish" was able to stir any personal interest in me other than a passing one, typical of any reader. "I'll Come Tomorrow" was the ironic tale of an unfaithful woman, of her failed deceit and the imbroglio that ensued. "The Goldfish", which was set in New York, was, strictly speaking, a dialogue between a man and a woman, with a description of a musical melody; a housemaid forgets to take a small goldfish bowl off the radiator, and the fish jump out of the hot water and thrash about on a rug, dying, while the participants of the dialogue fail to notice this, as she is engrossed in playing the piano, and he in listening to her playing. The story's interest lay in its introduction of a musical melody as a sentimental and irrefutable commentary, and in the unintentional participation of the fish in this, thrashing around on the rug.

I was struck, however, by the third story: "The Adventure in the Steppe". A line of Edgar Allan Poe's provided an epigraph to the tale: "Beneath me lay my corpse, with the arrow in my temple." This alone was sufficient to attract my attention. Although I cannot convey the sensation that gripped me as I read. The story concerned an episode from a war; it was written without any reference whatsoever to the country in which the narrative took place or to the nationality of those taking part in it, yet it would seem that the title alone, "The Adventure in the Steppe", suggested that it might have been set in Russia. It began thus: "The finest horse I ever owned was a white stallion, a half-breed of impressive dimensions, of note for its particularly broad, sweeping trot. It was so beautiful that I am inclined to compare it with those horses mentioned in the Book of Revelation. This similarity, incidentally, is highlighted—for me personally—by the fact that I rode this horse, galloping towards my own death, across the scorching earth, during one of the hottest summers I have ever known in my life."

Herein I found an exact reconstruction of everything I'd experienced during the far-distant times of the Civil War in Russia and a description of those unbearably hot days when the fiercest and most protracted fighting was taking place. Before long I reached the final pages of the story; I read them with bated breath. There I recognized my black mare and the turn in the road where she was killed. The narrator of the story was convinced from the outset that the rider who had fallen with his horse had been at least seriously wounded—since he had shot twice, and he thought that he had hit both times. I don't know why I noticed only a single shot. "But he was not dead, nor even apparently wounded," continued the author, "because I saw him stand up; in the bright sunlight I noticed what I thought to be the dark gleam of a revolver in his hand. He had no rifle—I know that much for sure."

15

The white stallion carried on at a heavy gallop, drawing nearer to the spot where, with an incomprehensible—as the author described it—immobility, paralysed perhaps by fear, stood a man with a revolver in his hand. The author then checked the horse's swift pace and shouldered his rifle, but suddenly, without hearing the shot, he felt a deathly pain he knew not where and a burning mist in his eyes. After a while, consciousness returned to him for a short, spasmodic moment, and it was then that he heard the slow steps approaching him; just as quickly, however, he fell back into oblivion. Again, after some time, finding himself already in a dying state of delirium, he—it's unimaginable how—sensed the presence of someone standing over him.

"I made a superhuman effort to open my eyes and see, at last, my death. So many times had I dreamt of its terrible iron face that I could never mistake it; time and again I would have recognized those features, known to me down to the smallest detail. But now I was astonished to see above me a youthful, pale face, completely unfamiliar to me, with distant, tired—or so they seemed to me—eyes. It was a boy of probably fourteen or fifteen, with a commonplace, ugly little face that expressed nothing other than manifest fatigue. He stood thus for a few seconds, then placed his revolver back into its holster and walked off. When I opened my eyes again and with the last of my strength turned my head, I saw him astride my horse. Then I blacked out again, regaining consciousness only many days later, in a military hospital. The bullet from the revolver had hit my chest half a centimetre above my heart. My horse of the

Apocalypse hadn't quite succeeded in carrying me to the very end. However, I believe that it was not very far from death and that it continued onwards on its journey, just with a different rider on its back. I'd pay dearly for the chance to know where, when and how they both met their end, and whether that revolver was still of use to the boy as he shot at the spectre of death. I don't imagine him to have been a very good shot at all; he didn't have that air about him. That he hit me was most likely a fluke, but then again I'd be the last person to reproach him for this. I'd also refrain because I think he probably perished long ago, vanishing into oblivion, astride that white stallion, as the last phantom of this adventure in the steppe."

There remained little doubt for me that the author of the story really was that same pale stranger whom I'd shot. To explain the complete convergence of facts with all their inherent peculiarities—right down to the colour and description of the horses—by pure coincidence was, to my mind, impossible. I took another look at the cover: *I'll Come Tomorrow, by Alexander Wolf.* This, of course, could have been a pseudonym. But I wouldn't let that stop me; I was determined to meet this man. That he was an English writer was also surprising. True, Alexander Wolf could have been a compatriot of mine with a decent enough command of English not to have recourse to the aid of a translator; this was the most probable explanation. In any case, I wanted to clarify this at whatever the cost, because after all I'd been connected to this man too long and too inseparably, without knowing him at all, and his memory had pervaded my entire life. Besides, judging by his story, it was also clear that he ought to harbour almost the same interest towards me, namely because of "The Adventure in the Steppe" having had such a significant bearing on his life and, probably, having predetermined his fate to a greater degree than my memory of him had predetermined that evanescing shadow that had been cast over many years of my life.

I wrote a letter to him, care of his publisher in London. I outlined the facts unknown to him at the time and asked him to send me a response, stating where and when we could meet—if, of course, such a meeting interested him as much as it did me. A month passed without any reply. It was always possible that he'd thrown the letter into the waste-paper basket without reading it, supposing it to have been sent by some female fan of his, with a request for a signed photograph and asking his opinion on the correspondent's own novel, which she would send or even read to him personally, just as soon as she had received his reply. This seemed in some way probable also because, despite the undoubted and real artistry with which the book had been written, it did contain, I think, a particular appeal for women. For one reason or another, however, I received no answer.

Precisely two weeks after this, I came upon an unexpected opportunity to travel to London for a spot of reporting. I was there for three days and found the time to drop by the publishing house that had printed Alexander Wolf's book. The director received me. He was a corpulent man of around fifty, with an air of something between a banker and a professor. He spoke French fluently. I outlined to him the reason for my visit and told him in a few words that I had read "The Adventure in the Steppe" and why this story had interested me.

"I'd like to know whether Mr Wolf received my letter."

"Mr Wolf isn't in London at the moment," said the director, "and we, I'm afraid, are without the means by which to contact him right now."

"This is beginning to resemble a detective story," I said, not without some vexation. "I shan't abuse your time, leaving you instead with my best wishes. May I count on your reminding Mr Wolf of my letter, once you resume contact with him—that is, if that ever happens?"

"You may rest assured," he replied hurriedly. "But I would add one thing more. I understand that your interest in the identity of Mr Wolf is of an entirely benign nature. And so I ought to tell you that Mr Wolf cannot be the man you're looking for."

"I had, until now, been completely convinced of the contrary."

"No, no," he said. "Insofar as I understand, he's supposed to be a compatriot of yours."

"That would be the most likely scenario."

"In that case, it's quite out of the question. Mr Wolf is an Englishman; I've known him for many years and can vouch for that. What's more, he's never left England for more than two or three weeks at a time, which he spends mostly in France or Italy. He hasn't travelled farther; I can say this with certainty."

"Then this has all been a misunderstanding, although it does surprise me," I said.

"As far as 'The Adventure in the Steppe' is concerned, it's fictitious from first to last."

"That, ultimately, isn't impossible."

In the final moments of our conversation I stood up, preparing to leave. The director also rose from his chair and said suddenly, markedly lowering his voice:

"Naturally, 'The Adventure in the Steppe' is a work of fiction. But if it were true, then I can only say that you've acted with unforgivable carelessness. You ought to have taken better aim. It would have spared both Mr Wolf and certain other parties unnecessary difficulties."

I looked at him in astonishment. He wore a very forced smile, which seemed to me entirely misplaced.

"It's true, you were much too young, and the conditions excuse the inaccuracy of your aim. Then again, it's all, as far as Mr Wolf is concerned, merely a product of the imagination, which has by chance coincided with your reality. I wish you all the best. If I hear any news, I'll be sure to convey it to you. Permit me to add one more thing; I'm a dash sight older than you, and it seems to me that I have a certain right to do so. I can assure you that an acquaintance with Mr Wolf, were it to come about, would bring you nothing other than disappointment and would surely want for the interest you vainly ascribe to it."

This conversation could not but make an exceedingly strange impression on me. It was evident that the director of the publishing house had some personal score to settle with

Wolf and genuine—or indeed imaginary—reasons to hate him. His words of near reproach directed towards me on account of my inadequate marksmanship came unexpectedly from the lips of this stout, mild-mannered man. As the book had been published some two years previously, one had to suppose that the events causing the director to change his attitude towards Wolf had taken place in this space of time. All this, however, could scarcely impart to me the slightest impression of the author of the collection *I'll Come Tomorrow*; all I'd learnt was the director's negative opinion of him, an evidently biased one at that. I carefully read the book through once more; my impression didn't change: that same impetuous, taut rhythm, the precision of detail, that same unfaltering and seemingly everlasting unison of plot with very short, expressive authorial commentaries.

I cannot say that I reconciled myself to the impossibility of finding out what interested me about Wolf, but I simply didn't see how it could be done. A whole month had already passed since that strange conversation in London, and I hardly doubted that I ought not to count on a reply from Wolf—perhaps not ever, and in any case not in the near future. I very nearly stopped thinking about it entirely.

I was living completely alone at the time. Among the restaurants where I dined or breakfasted—there were four of them, in different parts of the city—was a small Russian restaurant, the closest to my apartment, and in which I could be found several times a week. I went there on Christmas Eve, at around ten o'clock. All the tables were taken, and there was only one space free—in the farthest corner, where alone sat a festively dressed elderly man, whom I knew well by sight, as he dined there frequently. He would always show up with different women; they were difficult to categorize in a few words, but, more often than not, their lives seemed to be characterized by some sort of hiatus in their vocation: if she were an actress, she was a former actress; if a singer, she had recently lost her voice; if a simple waitress, she was sure to have married a short while ago. He had a reputation for being something of a Don Juan, and I imagine that he probably did enjoy a certain degree of success among this circle of women. This was why I was particularly surprised to see him alone on such a day. One way or another, however, I was offered the empty seat at his table; I sat down opposite him and greeted him with a handshake, which I had never before had the opportunity of doing.

He was rather sombre; his eyes were beginning to grow dim. Once I'd seated myself, he drank three shots of vodka in quick succession and suddenly livened up. All around people were chatting loudly, and the restaurant's gramophone played one record after another. Just as he poured himself a fourth shot, the gramophone started playing a melancholy little French number:

> *Il pleut sur la route,*
> *Le cœur en déroute.*

He listened closely, tilting his head to one side. When the record reached the words:

Malgré le vent, la pluie,
Vraiment si tu m'aimes…

his eyes actually welled with tears. Only then did I realize
that he was awfully drunk already.

"This song," he began in an unexpectedly loud voice,
turning to me, "brings back a few memories."

I noticed that next to him, on the little divan where he
was sitting, lay a book wrapped in paper, which he kept
moving from place to place, obviously taking care not to
crease it.

"I'd imagine you have a good few 'memories'."

"Why do you say that?"

"You have that air about you, I think."

He laughed and admitted that he did indeed have quite
a few "memories"; he had been seized by a fit of candour
and a need to talk, a characteristic particularly common to
inebriates of his sprawling sort. He began relating to me
his amorous adventures, although in many cases it seemed
clear that they had been either dreamt up or exaggerated.
I was, however, pleasantly surprised that he did not speak
ill of a single one of his many victims; each of his recollections contained something like a mix of debauchery and
tenderness. It was a very particular nuance of feeling, a trait
of his; indeed there was an undoubted and inadvertent
attractiveness in him, and so I came to realize just how this
man, in fact, could have enjoyed success with many women.
Despite the avid attention I paid to his story, I couldn't
commit faithfully to memory the random and disorderly

string of women's names he cited. Then he sighed, interrupting himself mid-flow, and said:

"But never in my life was there anyone better than my little Gypsy, Marina."

When speaking of women, he would frequently employ diminutive terms—"the little Gypsy", "the little blonde", "the little brunette", "the little quick one"—so much so that, as an outsider to the conversation, one gained the distinct impression that he was talking about a group of minors.

He described Marina to me at length. According to him, she was possessed of absolutely all those virtues that in themselves are exceedingly rare; what seemed most astonishing of all, however, was that she rode better than any jockey and fired a gun without ever missing a shot.

"Why then did you decide to part company with her?" I asked.

"It wasn't I who decided, my friend," he said. "My little swarthy one left me, but she didn't go far—only next door, to my neighbour. Here you go"—he showed me the book in its wrapping—"she left me for him, would you believe?"

"For the author of this book?"

"Whom else?"

"May I?" I said, reaching out a hand.

"Be my guest."

I removed the wrapping—and my eyes were suddenly struck by a familiar combination of letters: *I'll Come Tomorrow, by Alexander Wolf.*

It was as unexpected as it was astonishing. I was

dumbstruck for a good few seconds, just staring at the title. Then I asked:

"Are you sure that the shop assistant hasn't made a mistake and handed you something else by accident?"

"My good man," he said, "whatever mistake can there be here? I may not read English, but rest assured there's no mistake."

"I know this book, but I was recently told that its author was an Englishman."

He again began to laugh.

"Sasha Wolf, an Englishman! Damn it, you might as well tell me he's Japanese."

"Sasha Wolf, you say?"

"Yes, Sasha Wolf. Alexander Andreyevich, if you will. As English as you and I."

"Do you know him well?"

"I'll say!"

"Has it been long since you last saw him?"

"Last year," he said, helping himself to some vodka. "Your good health. Last year, around this very time. We really cut loose in Montmartre then and spent two whole days there. I can't even remember what happened or how I got home. It's the same every time he comes to Paris. I, as you know, have no aversion to drinking or—how should I say?—enjoying myself, but he's something else. I'll say to him, 'Steady on, Sasha,' but he always gives the same response. 'We've only got one shot at life,' he says, 'and it's a bad one at that, so what the hell?' What can you say to that? You can only agree with him."

By now he was utterly drunk; he was beginning to slur his speech.

"So you mean to say that he doesn't live in Paris?"

"Yes, he's mostly in England, although he does get around. I ask him, 'Why don't you write in Russian, damn it? We'd give it a read.' He says there's no point: it's more profitable to do it in English, it's better paid."

"So what happened with Marina?"

"Do you have the time?"

"In abundance."

He then began to relate to me, in every detail, the story of Marina, of Alexander Wolf, of when and how it all happened. It was a chaotic if rather colourful narrative, which was broken every now and then by his drinking now to Wolf's health, now to Marina's. He spoke a great deal and at length, and, despite it lacking any semblance of chronological order, I was able to construct a more or less coherent idea of it.

Alexander Wolf was younger than this man—whose name was Vladimir Petrovich Voznesensky, a person of ecclesiastical extraction—by five or six years. He was from Moscow, or possibly from somewhere else, but from the north of Russia in any case. Voznesensky had met him in a cavalry regiment under the command of Comrade Ofitserov, a leftist revolutionary with a penchant for anarchism. The regiment was waging a partisan war in southern Russia.

"Against whom?" I asked.

"Against any forces that were trying to seize illegitimate power," said Voznesensky with unexpected resolve.

Insofar as I understood, Comrade Ofitserov had not been pursuing any definite political goal. He was one of those archetypal adventurers, renowned in the annals of every revolution and every civil war. His regiment's numbers now increased, now decreased, depending upon circumstances, the degree of difficulties they were facing, the time of year and a multitude of other, often chance, reasons. But the core of his group always remained the same, and Alexander Wolf was Ofitserov's right-hand man. He was, according to Voznesensky, distinguished for a number of qualities, typical in such fables: unerring bravery, tirelessness, the ability to drink vast quantities of alcohol, as well as being, of course, a good comrade. He spent over a year in Ofitserov's regiment. During this time they had to live in the most varied conditions: in peasant huts and manor houses, in fields and in the forest; sometimes they went hungry for days at a time, sometimes they gorged themselves; they suffered from the cold in winter and from the heat in summer—in short, they experienced what is known to almost anyone who participates in a war of whatever length. Wolf in particular was always smartly turned out and well presented. "To this day I don't know where he found the time to shave every day," said Voznesensky. He could play the piano and drink pure spirits; he loved women and never played cards. He also knew German, as became apparent one day when he and Voznesensky came upon some German settlers. An old woman, the mistress of the farm, who spoke no Russian, planned to send her daughter by cart to the next town, three kilometres away, to inform the headquarters of the

Soviet division there that there were two armed partisans in the village. She said all this to her daughter in German, in the presence of Voznesensky and Wolf.

"What happened next?"

"He didn't say anything at that point; we just detained the girl, tied her up and took her to the attic. Then we gathered up the provisions and left."

According to Voznesensky, Wolf, when leaving, shook his head and said, "What an old crone, eh?" "Why didn't you shoot her?" asked Voznesensky later, when Wolf was explaining to him what had happened. "Damn her to hell," said Wolf. "She doesn't have that much longer left to live; God will deal with her without any help from you or me."

Wolf had been very lucky during the war; he managed to walk away completely unharmed from even the most dangerous of situations.

"He wasn't ever wounded?" I asked.

"Only once," said Voznesensky. "But so seriously that I began making preparations for the funeral. It isn't a *façon de parler*, as the French say; the doctor announced that Sasha had only a few hours to live."

The doctor, however, was mistaken; Voznesensky put it down to his having underestimated Wolf's resilience. Voznesensky added that Wolf had been wounded in completely mysterious circumstances, about which he was never disposed to say anything, alleging that he did not remember how it had happened. At the time there had been bitter fighting between elements of the Red Army and the retreating Whites; Ofitserov's division would hide in the forests and steer clear of this entirely. Almost an hour after the firing fell silent, Wolf announced that he was going on a reconnaissance mission and rode off alone. Around an hour and a half passed without his return. Voznesensky and two of his comrades set off in search of him. A little while before, they had heard three shots: the third had been farther off and weaker than the first two. They covered almost three kilometres of empty road; all was quiet, with no one in sight. The heat was searing. Voznesensky was the first to see Wolf: he was lying immobile across the road and "coughing up blood and foam", as Voznesensky described it. Wolf's horse was missing, which was also surprising; it usually followed him around like a dog and would never have gone off of its own free will.

"Do you remember what the horse was like, what colour it was?"

Voznesensky sank into thought, and then said:

"No, I don't recall. God knows, it was a long time ago. So much has happened since then."

"But you say the horse followed him around like a dog?"

"He had a knack for it," said Voznesensky. "All his horses were like that. You know, there are those whom even the most vicious dogs won't touch. He had that same gift with horses."

The circumstances in which Wolf was so gravely wounded seemed particularly odd to both Voznesensky and his comrades. The doctor said later that the injury was the result of a bullet wound from a revolver, and that the shot had been made at such close quarters that Wolf must have seen the man who shot him. Most of all, it was strange that there had been no struggle, nor had there been anyone else around; only, not far from the spot where they found Wolf lay a dead black mare, still with its saddle on. Voznesensky concluded that it must have been the mare's owner who had shot Wolf, and that he had ridden off on Wolf's horse. He added that if they—Voznesensky and his companions—had arrived in time, they wouldn't have begrudged the bullet to avenge their comrade. I recalled the rush of warm air that had carried the clatter of horses' hooves to me—that same sound that had caused me to leave immediately.

"But perhaps, ultimately," Voznesensky said unexpectedly, "the fellow was just defending his own life and isn't to blame. I propose, therefore, a toast to his health. You need another drink; you've got a very pensive look about you."

I silently nodded my head. A deep female voice came singing from the gramophone:

> There's no need for anything,
> Not even late regrets...

It was already past midnight, and the air hung with the cool scent of champagne, little cloudlets of perfume; there was also a smell of roast goose and baked apples. The noise of muffled automobile horns drifted in from the street; on the other side of the restaurant window, separated from us by glass alone, a winter's night was beginning, with the washed-out, cold light from the street lamps reflected on the wet Parisian road. With an inexplicably dismal clarity, I saw before me that hot summer's day, the cracked black-grey road, lazily, as if in a dream, winding through the little groves, and Wolf's motionless body, lying on the hot earth after that mortal fall.

Voznesensky took Wolf to a little white-and-green town on the Dnieper—white from the colour of the houses, green from the trees—and brought him to the hospital. The doctor told Voznesensky that Wolf had a matter of hours to live. After three weeks, however, Wolf walked out of the hospital with sunken cheeks and a thick bristle on his face, making him quite unrecognizable. Voznesensky had come to collect him with Marina, a girl whom he'd met the day after his arrival in the town. She wore an airy white dress, and there were bracelets jangling about her swarthy arms. She had fled her family around two years prior to this, and since then had been travelling all over southern Russia, earning a living by fortune-telling and singing. Voznesensky staunchly believed that she lived solely on those two sources of income; judging by his description of her, however, I doubt she would have had much cause to worry about her daily subsistence. She was seventeen or eighteen at the time. There was a noticeable change in Voznesensky's voice whenever he spoke of her, and I'd wager that had he not been quite so drunk he wouldn't have divulged to me certain completely unrepeatable yet truly rare qualities of Marina's, about which, of course, only those who had often experienced the irresistible, burning charm of her intimacy could know. Voznesensky lived with Marina in a modest villa; Wolf, who was still too weak to take up his former partisan life again, installed himself two doors down from them. Voznesensky's house had a piano. The following day, dressed in civilian clothes, neat and shaved as always, Wolf paid a visit to his comrade; they dined together, and later Wolf sat down at the piano and began to accompany Marina, who had been singing.

Some time afterwards, Voznesensky left to visit Ofitserov for a few days, and when he returned Marina was gone. He went to Wolf's, and she opened the door to him. Wolf was not at home that day. She looked at Voznesensky without any embarrassment whatsoever, and with a savage and direct ease told him that she no longer loved him, but loved Sasha instead. Voznesensky said that at that moment she had been just like Carmen.

"I was a hardened man," he said. "I'd seen my comrades killed before my very eyes, I myself had often risked my life, and everything had washed over me like water off a duck's back. But that day I went home, lay down on my bed and cried like a little boy."

What he then told me was both astounding and naive. He tried to convince Marina that Wolf was still too weak, that she ought to have taken pity on him and left him in peace.

"Well, I'll leave him when he starts coughing and wheezing," she answered with that same characteristic ease.

Nevertheless, Marina's betrayal did not affect relations between Voznesensky and Wolf. Voznesensky even found it within himself to remain on good terms with Marina. She lived with Wolf for a number of months, accompanied the regiment everywhere, and only then did they see her skill in the saddle and with a gun.

Then terrible times befell them. A cavalry division was sent in pursuit of the regiment, whose numbers had dwindled to two hundred men. They spent weeks hiding in the forests. This was in the Crimea. Ofitserov was killed. On one of their last days there they came upon some recently abandoned, well-equipped dugouts in the forest. For the first time in a week and a half they passed a peaceful night, in relative warmth and with a handful of comforts. They slept for hours on end. When they awoke late the next morning Marina was gone.

"We never found out what happened to her," said Voznesensky, "or where she wound up."

However, there was neither the time nor the opportunity to search for her. They reached the coast on foot, and left Russia in the hold of a Turkish coal steamer. After a fortnight they parted ways in Constantinople, only to meet again twelve years later in Paris, in a Métro carriage, when Wolf, not for the first time, had come over to France from England, where he was residing.

Thus Voznesensky never learnt anything of Marina's fate. She had appeared unexpectedly one summer's morning, on the market square of this little town on the Dnieper, and disappeared just as unexpectedly, at the dawn of an autumn day, in the Crimea. "She came, burned and vanished," he said. "But we never forgot her, neither Sasha nor I."

I looked at him and thought about the unlikely set of circumstances that tied my own life to everything he'd said.

Fifteen years ago this man, who was now sitting opposite me in a Parisian restaurant, celebrating Christmas Eve with some vodka, goose and reminiscences, while in the friendliest of dispositions towards me, had in fact ridden alongside his two comrades in search of Alexander Wolf, and were it not for a gentle breeze I wouldn't have heard their approach, and they might have caught up with me, and then, of course, my revolver wouldn't have saved me. True, I think that Wolf's white stallion would have been swifter than their horses, but it, too, could have been wounded or killed, like my black mare. This, however, did not occupy my thoughts for long. It was a random occurrence that was now affecting my fate, and if I were to be asked what would have been better, to be killed then or to be spared for the life that awaited me, I'm not entirely convinced that it would have been worth opting for the latter. Voznesensky and I finally parted; he walked off with an unsteady gait, and I was left alone, my mind laden with everything I'd learnt over the past, while stirring inside me a whole score of discordant and contradictory notions. Of course, there might have been a certain degree of fantasy in Voznesensky's tale, as is almost inevitable for any such oral memoir, but that did not alter the crux of the story. What I'd gleaned from the director of the publishing house came in sharp contrast to what I learnt from the conversation in the restaurant that evening; true, I was far less inclined to believe the director than my Christmas companion. But why then had he felt the need to convince me that Wolf never left England for long, and why had he lamented that

34

I hadn't killed him? These, however, were incidental considerations. Most surprising of all was something else entirely: just how could this Sasha Wolf—friend of Voznesensky's, adventurer, drunkard, philanderer, Marina's seducer—write *I'll Come Tomorrow*? The book's author couldn't be that man. I knew that it had to be an undoubtedly clever, exceedingly cultivated man, for whom culture was a thing of no little import; moreover, he had to be innately different to such a dear and reckless old soak like Voznesensky, and everyone of this sort in general. For example, I could scarcely imagine someone who felt so confident in those psychological transitions and nuances upon whose successful execution Wolf's prose was built as being the same man who tied up a German settler girl. That said, there was nothing entirely beyond the realms of possibility in all this, and besides, it had taken place many years ago. Yet it was patently obvious that this didn't tally with any rational impression of the author of *I'll Come Tomorrow*. As far as I was concerned, his nationality was inconsequential. What I wanted to know most of all, if we were to suppose that Voznesensky's story was on the whole true—something of which I had little doubt—was how Sasha Wolf, adventurer and partisan, had turned into the Alexander Wolf who wrote this book. It was difficult to square this in my mind: the rider astride a white stallion, racing towards his death, *that* death—a bullet from a revolver, at full gallop—and the author of this book, who selected a quotation from a work by Edgar Allan Poe for the epigraph. Sooner or later, I thought, I'll find out, and perhaps I'll be able to retrace from start to finish what has interested me so much: the history of this life in its double aspect. It might happen, or it might not. In any case, it was only worth speaking of in the future tense, and I couldn't imagine the circumstances under which I'd discover it, if indeed I was fated to discover it. I was unconsciously drawn to this man; aside from those reasons that seemed the most obvious and satisfactory in accounting for my interest in him, there was one other, no less important or less connected to my own fate. When I first thought of it, it seemed absurd. It was like a thirst for self-justification or a search for compassion, and I began to remind myself of a man who, having been sentenced to a certain punishment, naturally seeks out a group of others serving the same sentence. In other words, the fate of Alexander Wolf also interested me because I, too, had suffered my whole life from an extraordinarily persistent and indomitable case of split personality, one that I had tried to fight and that had poisoned my happiest hours. Perhaps, though, Alexander Wolf's supposed split personality was only imaginary and all those things that seemed contradictory in my impression of him were merely the various elements of an inherent spiritual harmony. But if this were so, I needed to understand how he'd managed to achieve such a favourable outcome and succeed where I for so long had consistently failed.

I remembered my record of failures well, even dating back to a time when the matter of my split personality was entirely benign and in no way seemed to foreshadow those catastrophic consequences it bore later on. It began with my being attracted to two opposing things in equal measure: on the one hand there was the history of art and culture, reading, to which I devoted much time, and a predilection for abstract problems; on the other, so excessive a love of sport and everything to do with the purely physical, muscular, animal world. I very nearly strained my heart lifting weights that were far too heavy for me, I spent almost half my life in sports grounds, I participated in many competitions, and until recently I preferred a football to any theatre production. I still harbour painful memories of the savage fights that were so typical of my youth, utterly devoid of any resemblance to sport. All this came to an end long ago, of course, although I still have two scars on my head. I recalled, as if in a dream, my classmates bringing me home caked in blood, my school uniform torn to pieces. This, however—much like the fact that I kept the company of thieves and those generally enjoying a brief period of liberty between one prison and the next—didn't seem to hold any particular significance, although even then one may infer something odd about an equal, unfaltering love for such differing things as Baudelaire's poetry and a brutal punch-up with some thug. Later on, all this acquired rather different forms; far from seeing any improvement, however, the discrepancy and sharp contradiction so characteristic of my life became all the more glaring as it continued. It was to be found between what I felt inwardly drawn towards and what I so vainly struggled against—the tumultuous and sensual root of my existence. It interfered with everything, it obscured those meditative faculties I valued above all else, it wouldn't allow me to see things as I ought to have seen them, distorting them in its crude yet indomitable refractions, and it compelled me to perform a number of deeds that I invariably came to regret later on. It induced me to like things whose aesthetic insignificance I knew full well, things clearly in poor taste, yet the strength of my attraction to them could only compare with the simultaneous disgust I inexplicably felt towards them.

The most lamentable result of this split personality, however, was my psychological relation to women. For a long time I caught myself watching—with greedy, almost foreign, eyes—the harsh, crude feminine face, in which even the most perceptive and unbiased of observers would vainly strive to find any form of inspiration. I couldn't help noticing how a woman would dress with provocative, invariable tastelessness, so much so that I'd be unable to imagine there being anything other than purely animal reflexes within her; nevertheless, her body's movement and her swaying hips would never fail to make an inconceivably strong impression on me. True, I never had anything in common with women of that sort; quite the opposite—when approaching them, my principal feeling would always be one of disgust. The other women who passed through my life belonged to an entirely different category; they comprised part of a world in which I was always supposed to live, but from which I was so continually dragged down. They brought out my finest feelings, I believe, but it was all tinged with a sort of listless delight, leaving me each time with a vague sense of dissatisfaction. It had always been so, and I knew nothing else. I suppose it was something like an instinct for self-preservation that prevented me from taking that final step, an unconscious understanding that if it were to happen, it would end in inner catastrophe. I often sensed, however, that this was close at hand, and I thought Fate, which had until now so fortuitously led me out of many difficult and often dangerous situations, had favoured me, creating, for a few short hours in my life, the semblance of a peaceful and almost abstract happiness, which afforded no room to this uncontrollable downward pull. It was as if a man, forever drawn towards an abyss, had lived his life in a country where there were neither mountains nor cliffs, and only the flat expanse of level plains.

Time went on and my life trudged slowly alongside it; I became accustomed to the reality of my existence as people grow used to, say, the pain of an incurable illness. But I could never entirely reconcile myself with the knowledge that my savage and sensual perception of the world would deprive me of so many spiritual possibilities, and that there were things I might comprehend theoretically, yet that would for ever remain inaccessible to me—the world of lofty emotions, for example, which I had known and loved my whole life. This knowledge was reflected in everything I did and embarked on; I always knew that the inner strength I ought to have been capable of in principle, and that others were within their rights to expect of me, would prove beyond me; it was for this reason that I did not ascribe much significance to practical matters, and why my life generally had been so accidental and inherently disordered. This even

39

predetermined my choice of profession: instead of devoting my time to literary endeavours—as I was disposed to do, but which required a significant investment of time and selfless effort—I took up journalism, sporadic at best and renowned for its arduous variety. Subject to requirements, I wrote about everything under the sun, from political articles to film reviews and sporting commentary. It required neither any particular effort nor any specialist knowledge, and besides, I would use a pseudonym or my initials, thus shirking any responsibility for what I wrote. It did, however, teach me a valuable lesson: practically none of those who bore the brunt of my criticism could ever bring themselves to agree with my review, and they all would feel a pressing need to explain my error to me personally. Sometimes I was faced with writing about things that fell far beyond the realms of my competency; this would happen when I stood in for a correspondent who had taken ill or left. Once, for example, all the obituaries were assigned to me; I wrote around half a dozen of them over a period of two weeks, because Bossuet, my colleague who usually dealt with them (with an uncommon zeal and a rare professional integrity), was laid up in bed with bilateral pneumonia. When I went to visit him, he gave me a wry smile, saying:

"I hope, my dear colleague, that you won't wind up writing my obituary. It would be the greatest act of sacrifice that we could rightly expect of you."

"My dear Bossuet," I said, "I promise you categorically that I won't write your obituary. I don't think anyone could do it better than you…"

The most astonishing thing was that Bossuet had indeed prepared his own obituary, which he showed to me. This document contained everything that had become so natural to me, all the genre's fine classical idioms: there we saw selfless toil and death in the line of duty, *"pareil à un soldat, il est mort au combat"*, an irreproachable past, the family's grief, *"que vont devenir ses enfants?"*, and so on.

My period of obituary-writing was particularly memorable on account of my sixth and final article being returned to me from the editorial office with the demand that I give greater prominence to the positive attributes of the deceased. It was all the more tricky as it concerned a politician who had died from progressive paralysis. His entire life had been remarkable for a striking consistency: a succession of shady dealings, spurious bank transactions and party betrayals; then there were the banquets, visits to the most notorious cabarets and the costliest brothels, and ultimately death resulting from some venereal disease. The piece had to be rushed; I sat working on it for a whole evening, unable to eat at my usual time. Having just composed the final line and dispatched the article off to compositing, I decided to stop by the Russian restaurant where I'd celebrated Christmas Eve. There, after the long hiatus, I encountered Voznesensky once again, sitting alone and sincerely glad to see me, as though an old acquaintance. He addressed me in a relaxed, intimate manner, as if we had known one another for many years; coming from Voznesensky, there was, of course, nothing shocking about this. He asked me where I had been and whether he would have to wait for another

41

of the Twelve Great Feasts to see me again. Then he took an interest in what I had been doing generally. When I told him that I was a journalist, he became particularly excited.

"That's a great blessing," he said. "God wasn't quite so benevolent to me."

"Why a great blessing?"

"My dear chap, if I were a journalist I'd write the sort of stuff that would leave the world astounded."

"I don't think it's necessary to be a journalist for that. You might try it sometime."

"I did," he replied. "Nothing came of it."

And so he told me how he once sat down to write his memoirs, wrote late into the night and was in raptures over how wonderfully everything was coming out.

"So clever, you know—such brilliant imagery, such a richness of style. It was simply staggering."

"Excellent," I said. "Why didn't you continue?"

"I lay down to sleep," he said. "Morning was already nigh. I was utterly blinded by this gift of mine, which had so suddenly revealed itself."

Then he sighed and added:

"But when I awoke and read everything over, I felt very disheartened, you know. Such was the nonsense, so idiotically was everything written, that I just washed my hands of the whole thing. I'll never write again."

He sat looking thoughtfully ahead; his face wore an expression of sincere disappointment. Then, as if remembering something, he asked me:

"Oh, yes, that's what I was meaning to talk to you about.

Tell me, what did you make of Sasha's book? Does he write well, or just so-so? You remember, Sasha Wolf, whom we spoke about?"

I voiced my thoughts on the matter. He shook his head.

"And he doesn't mention Marina in the book?"

"No."

"A pity, she would have been worth it. So, what does he write about? You must forgive me for interrogating you like this. I don't know any English, so Sasha's book just lies there at home like a manuscript in some mysterious tongue."

I gave him an abridged account of the book's contents. He was, of course, particularly interested in "The Adventure in the Steppe". Nevertheless, he could not reconcile himself to the idea that Sasha Wolf—that same Sasha whom he knew so well, "a man just like any other"—had turned out to be a writer, and an English one at that.

"Where did all this spring from? It's beyond me," he said. "That's talent for you. No more or less a man than I, and yet I've wasted my whole life on trifles, whereas they'll write articles and even, maybe, books about Sasha. Perhaps we'll be remembered if he mentions us in his writing; in fifty years' time pupils in England will read about us, and so everything that has happened won't have been in vain."

He looked straight ahead, with an unseeing gaze.

"And so everything will live on," he continued, thinking aloud. "How the bracelets jangled around Marina's arms, what the Dnieper was like that summer, how scorching the heat was, and how Sasha had lain across the road. So he did see who shot him, then? From the description, it was a young lad, you say? What exactly did he say about him?"

I retold that part of the story in greater detail.

"Yes, indeed," said Voznesensky. "That sounds about right. He took fright, perhaps, the boy. Can you imagine? His horse was killed right under him—he's standing, the poor chap, alone in a field, while some bandit with a rifle comes racing towards him."

He sank back into thought.

"We'll never find out anything about him, then. Was he a schoolboy who not so long ago had sat at home, reading his mother's books and being more terrified of his teacher than a machine gun? Or was he a ruffian, a waif? And did he shoot from fear or with the cold calculation of a murderer? In any case," he added unexpectedly, "if I, by some miracle, were to meet him, I'd say to him: 'Thank you, my boy, for shooting wide of the mark; because of that, we're all still alive: Marina, Sasha and even, perhaps, I.'"

"You credit it with such significance?"

"Why not?" he said. "Life goes by without leaving a trace: millions of people disappear, and no one remembers them. And of these millions only the smallest handful remains. What could be more remarkable? Or look at it this way: take a beautiful woman, like Marina, for whom dozens of people are even prepared to die—a few years and there'll be nothing left of her other than a rotting corpse. Now is that really fair?"

"Truly, one can only pity that you aren't a writer."

"Ah, my dear friend, of course. And you thought I was grieved about this for no good reason! I'm a simple

44

man, but what's to be done if the thirst for immortality resides within me? I've led a very rakish life—all girls and restaurants—but it doesn't mean that I've never given serious thought to anything. Quite the contrary, after the girls and restaurants, in peace and solitude, that's when you remember everything, and when it rests especially heavily on the heart. Any libertine or drunkard can tell you this."

Now he was in a contemplative mood and was almost sober. He eventually adopted a tone that elders sometimes use when speaking to their juniors: "When you've lived as long as I have…", "You, of course, are too young…" The conversation then returned to Wolf, but Voznesensky revealed nothing new about him.

Several more weeks passed by, and in all this time nothing was added to my knowledge, even as far as my own speculations were concerned. I didn't receive a single letter from London. More than once, the thought crossed my mind that the situation might for ever remain at this impasse: Wolf might die, I might never meet him, and my sum knowledge of him would be confined to "The Adventure in the Steppe", my personal recollections of those torrid summer days and what Voznesensky had told me. Again I would recall the road, the white-and-green town on the Dnieper, the sounds of the piano in the little villa, and the jangling from the bracelets around Marina's arms—then everything would gradually fade and grow dark, and finally almost nothing would remain, except, perhaps, for the book written in that taut, precise language, whose title sounded to me like distant mockery.

I continued to frequent the restaurant from time to time, although my visits never coincided with Voznesensky's. He had, however, lost a significant portion of my interest. The gramophone connected to the radio apparatus played its records as usual, and every time the deep woman's voice began the song:

> There's no need for anything,
> Not even late regrets…

I would involuntarily raise my head and imagine the door swinging open and Voznesensky walking in, swiftly followed by a man with fair hair and the fixed gaze of those grey eyes. I now remembered clearly that he had grey eyes, despite their being clouded over by the approach of death when I first saw them; I noticed their colour only because it had taken place in such exceptional circumstances.

The mode of my life remained as it always had been. Nothing about it changed; everything was, as ever, chaotic and unhappy. At times I was unable to detach myself from the impression that I had been living like this for an endless length of time and, to the point of deathly ennui, had already witnessed all that I was destined to see: this city, these cafés and cinemas, these newspaper offices, the same conversations about the same things with practically the same people. Then, one day in February, during a mild and rainy winter, without forewarning or anticipation of anything new, events were set in motion that, as a result, were to take me a great distance. In fact, their origin cannot in any way be put down to chance, at least not as far as I am concerned. Just as I had been writing obituaries some time ago, filling in for Bossuet (who had now, thankfully, regained his health and, with unaccountable zeal, once again taken up writing his lyrical obituaries), so now I was to stand in for another colleague, a sports correspondent who had gone to Barcelona to attend a highly important—as far as he was concerned—international football match. The day after this, a no less significant event was to take place in Paris, namely the light-heavyweight world championship final, and I had been entrusted to cover the fight. The outcome of the match greatly interested me. I had a complete overview of the careers and respective merits of both opponents, and their clash held a particular appeal. One of the boxers was a Frenchman, the renowned Émile Dubois; the other was an American, Fred Johnson, whose European debut this was. Dubois was the popular favourite. I was among the few who thought that Johnson would win the match; I had information at my disposal that was unknown to the major-ity of the public and even that of journalists, and so I had grounds on which to base my theory. I had long known of Dubois; over the last few years he hadn't lost a single match. Despite this, however, he was not what could be called an outstanding boxer. He had an undoubted natural ability, but this was due more to the absence of certain faults than the sum of his merits: he was noted for having exceptional

47

stamina, he could withstand an onslaught of ferocious blows, his heart and lungs were excellent, and he was able to maintain a constant, steady control over his breathing. Those were his positive traits, but they were insufficient to aver any keen professional originality. The tactics he employed—always the same—testified to a complete lack of imagination and creativity; they had proven successful a couple of times, and so thereafter he never altered them. He had short arms, and he was neither quick nor agile enough. He won his matches through frequent *corps à corps*, his blows always struck at his opponent's ribs, and he only had two top-class knockouts to his career—both complete flukes. He had cauliflower ears, and a disjointed nose from taking direct hits; he usually charged at his opponent like a bull, dropping his strong head and enduring the barrage of blows with unquestionable, blind bravery. He was the European light-heavyweight champion, and on this occasion all the papers predicted a swift victory for him. In his private life he was a stupid but extremely kind-hearted man. Incidentally, he never levelled any complaints against journalists, regardless of what they wrote about him, and anyway, to top it all off, he read with difficulty and took little interest in what the papers said.

As far as Fred Johnson was concerned, I knew only what the American press had written about him. It required a great effort to extract from the mass of publicity pieces any real information by which to judge him. Johnson had been unable to complete his university studies because he lacked the necessary funds, and it was precisely this that caused him to choose boxing as a profession. That in itself was odd enough. A second peculiarity of his—without doubt purely professional—was that he carried almost all his matches right through to the final round. A third, which nearly everyone who wrote about him found cause to lament, was that he lacked the necessary power behind his punch, leaving the number of knockouts in his career negligible. Still, they would occur every now and then, causing general amazement each time, but since it happened so rarely it was always soon forgotten. All those who wrote about him, without exception, remarked on the unusual speed of his movements and the variety of his tactics. I had seen his photograph many times: Johnson's face, as opposed to the majority of other boxers' faces, bore no trace of disfigurement. Reading through a few dozen articles about him and charting the results of his matches, I drew a few, purely theoretical, conclusions, which I was now intent on proving. My conclusions were as follows: firstly, Johnson was intelligent, at least as far as boxing was concerned, and this gave him an instant sizeable advantage over his opponent. (I greatly admire boxing, but I've long been convinced that nine times out of ten any illusions as to a boxer's presence of mind or his having even an elementary degree of ingenuity, if only in the technical sense, are completely baseless.) Secondly, Johnson evidently possessed no less stamina than Dubois, since only a boxer with exceptional physical ability could allow himself the luxury of holding out for ten or fifteen rounds each time. Thirdly, he had mastered the technique of defence—the evidence being that, despite this career in boxing, his face had escaped relatively untouched. Lastly, and most importantly, he did indeed seem to have the requisite power behind his punch to deliver a knockout when absolutely necessary, but used it only on exceedingly rare occasions, preferring to win his matches on points. Also, he was younger than Dubois by six years; this too bore a certain significance.

I was confident that my conclusions were correct; however, they were based on unreliable secondary sources, such as sporting reports in American newspapers are wont to be. Johnson's challenge in this match came down to one thing only: that he ought to hold Dubois at a distance and avoid *corps à corps*. I was sure that Johnson would recognize this necessity and that, on that basis, his technical superiority should secure him the match.

It had been a long time since I last saw such a crowd or such a mass of motor cars as I did on the evening of the match, in front of the entrance to the enormous Palais des Sports. Tickets were sold out far in advance. The American ambassador's colossal vehicle was parked right in front of the Palais. Outside, a multitude of people thronged under the fine winter drizzle; the odd ticket tout could be seen hiding from the police in some dark corner. I'd hardly taken a few steps when an acquaintance of mine called out to me; he was a young architect whom I knew from my student days in the Latin Quarter.

"You lucky devil!" he shouted, shaking my hand. "You don't need to find some scoundrel to sell you a twenty-franc ticket for a hundred and fifty francs! Damn it, I need to get a press pass, just like you. Are you betting against Dubois? I'm down for ten francs. Oh, there he is!" he shouted, spotting a little man in a cap. "There's my ticket! See you later." And with that, he vanished.

That instant, with only a hint of a foreign accent, a female voice said to me very calmly and flatly:

"Excuse me, but are you really a journalist?"

I turned around. Standing in front of me was a woman of around twenty-five or twenty-six, well dressed, with small grey eyes and a rather beautiful, placid face. The style of her hat accentuated her clear, well-shaped forehead. I was astonished that she had approached a total stranger; it seemed out of character. However, she spoke so freely and with such ease that I immediately replied that, yes, indeed I was a journalist, and would be glad if I could be of some assistance to her.

"I couldn't get a ticket for the match," she said. "I'd really love to see it. Couldn't you get me in?"

"I'll try," I answered. In the end, after lengthy talks with the management and having bribed the ticket inspector, we were both admitted to the hall. I offered her my seat, which she accepted without any embarrassment, while I remained standing beside her, next to a concrete barrier that separated our seats from some others. Never once thereafter did she even glance at me. Before the match began, barely turning her head, she asked me:

"Who do you think will win?"

"Johnson," I said.

By then, however, the boxers were already in the ring,

and so the conversation ended there. The two fights preceding the championship match had been of no interest whatsoever. Finally, the moment had arrived when the main event was ready to begin. I glimpsed the broad, stocky figure of Dubois in a dark-pink Turkish robe; he approached the ring, accompanied by his manager and two others brandishing towels. His placid, vacant face wore that typical apathetic smile. The crowd applauded and cheered; shouts of encouragement could be heard from above:

"*Vas-y, Mimile! Fais lui voir! Tape dedans! T'as qu'à y aller franchement!*"

I failed to notice Johnson approaching the ring. He literally slid under the ropes and sprang up next to Dubois. As occasionally happens, a single random movement (in this instance, how he bent under the ropes and then straightened up again) can reveal how a whole body is possessed of a perfectly balanced range of movement. Johnson wore a navy-blue robe with vertical stripes. Once they disrobed, the difference between them became immediately apparent. Dubois seemed much broader and heavier than his opponent. Again, I saw his round, strong shoulders, his hairy chest and thick, muscular legs. With Johnson, I was struck first and foremost by how lean he was—his protruding ribs, and arms and legs that seemed especially thin in comparison to Dubois's. However, on closer inspection I saw that he had an immense ribcage, broad shoulders, legs of almost balletic beauty, and, on his hairless torso, his modest, flat muscles moved freely and obediently under his glistening skin. He had blond hair and an ugly, animated face. To look at, one would have supposed him to be around nineteen years old; he was, in fact, twenty-four. The audience applauded him too, but not, of course, as they had done Dubois. He bowed without smiling. At the sound of the gong, the match commenced.

I was immediately alarmed that Johnson's defensive position, similar to Dempsey's classical stance (both fists almost at eye level), was clearly unsuited to a match against Dubois, as it left his torso completely open. After the first round, however, I realized my mistake: Johnson's true defence lay not in one stance or another, but in the rare speed of his movements. Dubois opened the match at a blistering pace, which was out of character for him; he had evidently bowed to the advance instructions of his manager. One could see that he had trained superbly; never had I seen him on such perfect form. From where I was standing I had a clear view of the relentless barrage of blows, and I could hear their dull, pounding sound, similar from afar to the soft, uneven thud of hooves. They landed on Johnson's exposed chest; he drew back, circling the ring. Dubois's attack had been so unremitting that the public fixed their attention solely on him. No one, it seemed, was thinking about Johnson: "He's not there, he's not in the ring, I can't see even see his shadow!"—"It's not a match, it's a massacre!" screeched one woman's voice. Spurred on by the crowd, Dubois bore down on his opponent all the more fervently; you could see his round, energetic shoulders, the heavy, repetitive movements of his massive legs, and from an outsider's point of view it began to seem as though any resistance to this living, breathing, unstoppable machine was out of the question. The whole crowd thought likewise, and even the odd spectator, managing to keep his cool and follow the fight attentively, had to be of the same opinion.

"It's always the way with Americans," shouted my neighbour. "They work miracles in America, but they're given a drubbing in Europe!"

Because of the incredible speed with which the first round seemed to pass, I could not judge to what degree Johnson had the upper hand. Only during the time-out did I notice that he was breathing calmly and evenly, and on his face was that same intense, assured expression that I remembered from his photographs in the newspapers.

The second and third rounds were re-enactments of the first. I had never thought Dubois capable of such a swift, fierce attack, but it was already clear that he would be unable to achieve his sought-after *corps à corps*, from which Johnson would constantly back away. Dubois kept striving for it and spared no energy. His body glistened with sweat, but the blows kept falling with that same rhythm, never abating even for a minute. Johnson was continually drawing back, making almost full circles around the ring. At the end of the fourth round, it seemed as though the match had been decisively won and all that remained were a few formalities for a final ruling—the blows had continued to rain down on Johnson, who, by some miracle, was still standing: "*Coup de grâce! Coup de grâce!*" shouted shrill voices from above. "*T'as qu'à en finir, Mimile!*" Then, suddenly, there was a movement in the ring, like lightning, so quick that literally no one managed to catch it; the instant thud of a falling body rang out, and I saw that Dubois had gone crashing down with all his weight to the ground. It was so unexpected and so inconceivable that the noise from the crowd—a monstrous, simultaneous groan—swept through the whole of the enormous Palais des Sports. Even the referee was so taken aback that he did not immediately begin the count. At the count of seven, Dubois's body was still motionless. At eight, the sound of the gong rang out, declaring the end of the round.

From the fifth round onwards, the match acquired a completely different character. Just as until the fourth interval it had seemed as though only Dubois was in the ring, so now it was with Johnson. Only then was it possible to assess Johnston's extraordinary qualities. It was a masterclass in first-rate boxing, and Johnson was the unmistakable teacher, incapable of making a single error. Moreover, he was clearly going easy on his opponent. Dubois, half stunned, moved almost blindly, invariably running into Johnson's fists. He fell many more times, but would always get up with that same incredible strength of his. Towards the end, he almost gave up defending himself, covering his face helplessly with his hands, and, with his typical (and now barely conscious) courage, endured every blow. One of his eyes was swollen, and blood was trickling down his face; he licked it away mechanically, audibly gulping down his saliva. It was unclear why the referee didn't put a stop to the match. A few times in the middle of the round Johnson raised his arms, looking questioningly now at Dubois, now at the referee, and I distinctly heard him say: "But he's dead."

However, he shrugged his shoulders and continued with the now unnecessary demonstration of his amazing art. Only at the beginning of the sixth round, with that same quick movement, but this time seen by everyone, did his right fist strike Dubois's chin with an almighty power and precision; Dubois was carried out of the ring unconscious. A great cry went up in the room, amorphous and incoherent, and the crowd began slowly to disperse.

The winter rain poured down unceasingly. My companion and I stepped out into the street; I hailed a taxi and asked her where she was going.

"You've been so kind," she said, already sitting inside, with the door still open. "I don't know how to thank you."

"How about a cup of coffee? It's good for you after intense excitement," I said. She agreed, and we set off for an all-night café on rue Royale. Raindrops beat against the car windows, dimly glinting in the light from the street lamps.

"Why did you think Johnson would win the match?" she asked. I explained my reasoning to her in detail.

"You follow the American papers?"

"It's a professional requirement of mine."

She was silent. For some reason, I felt ill at ease in her presence, and I began to regret inviting her to the café. Whenever the taxi drove under a shaft of light from a street lamp, I saw her cold, placid face, and after a few minutes I began to think about my true reasons behind going for coffee with this unknown woman who wore such an absent expression, as though she were sitting in a hairdresser's or in a carriage on the Métro.

"For a journalist you're not very talkative," she said after some time.

"I gave you a detailed account of why I thought Johnson would win the match."

"And therein concludes your ability to make conversation?"

"I've no idea which topics interest you. I'd assumed it was boxing, mainly."

"Not always," she said, and at that moment the car came to a halt. A minute later we were sitting at a table, drinking coffee. Only then could I duly examine my companion, or, rather, I noticed one of her peculiarities: she had a surprisingly large mouth, with full, insatiable lips, and this gave her face a disharmonious appearance, as if there were something artificial about it, since the combination of her forehead and the lower portion formed a rather painful impression of some anatomical mistake. But when she smiled for the first time, baring her even rows of teeth and slightly opening her mouth, an expression of warm, sensual charm, which only a second ago would have seemed entirely impossible, suddenly flashed across her face. Later, I often recalled how it was precisely at that moment when I stopped feeling uncomfortable in her presence—something that had bound me thus far. I felt at ease. I questioned her about a variety of personal matters. She said that her surname was Armstrong, that her husband had recently died, and that she lived alone in Paris.

"Your husband was?…"

She replied that he had been an American, an engineer, and that she hadn't seen him in two years: she had been

57

in Europe, whereas he had stayed on in America. While in London she received a telegram informing her of his sudden death.

"You don't speak with an American accent," I remarked. "You have a neutrally foreign accent, if I might put it that way."

Once again she smiled that smile that always exuded an air of surprise and replied that she was Russian. I almost fell off my chair. To this day, I cannot fathom why it had seemed so astonishing to me.

"So you hadn't the slightest inclination that you were dealing with a compatriot?" She now spoke with a very pure Russian accent.

"You must admit that it would have been a radical assumption to make."

"And yet I knew that you were Russian."

"I bow to your perspicacity. And just how did you know, if it's no secret?"

"By your eyes," she said mockingly. Then she shrugged her shoulders and added, "Because there was a Russian newspaper sticking out of your coat pocket."

It was already past one o'clock. I offered to see her home. She replied that she would go alone, that she did not want to trouble me.

"No doubt your professional obligations are calling you."

"Yes, I ought to hand in my report on the match."

I was determined not to ask her where she lived or to seek out any more meetings with her. We left together; I walked her to a taxi and said:

"Good night. Goodbye."

A few drops of rain fell onto her hand as she offered it out to me. Smiling for one last time, she replied:

"Good night."

I am unsure whether it happened like this in reality, or whether it just seemed so to me. I detected in her voice a fleeting new intonation, a sort of audible smile, which had the same effect as that first, distantly sensual, movement of her lips and teeth, after which I stopped feeling uneasy in her presence. Without a moment's thought for the words coming out of my mouth, and, as if it had never happened, completely forgetting the decision I'd only just taken not to ask her anything, I said:

"I'd be sorry to say goodbye without knowing your name or your address. After all, if you really are interested in sport, perhaps I might be of further use to you."

"Possibly," she said. "My name is Yelena Nikolayevna. I'll give you my address and telephone number. Aren't you going to write it down?"

"No, I'll remember it."

"You trust your memory that much?"

"Absolutely."

She said she was at home until one o'clock in the afternoons, and in the evenings from seven until nine, then she slammed the door shut and the taxi drove off.

I walked towards the printing offices. It was a rather misty night, and the rain refused to abate for a single moment. I strolled along with the collar of my coat upturned, thinking of a great many things at once.

"Johnson's significance, which had until now seemed questionable, emerged last night so indisputably that now the matter has been settled once and for all. This was only to be expected, however, and to a few journalists, having at their disposal certain information regarding the career of the new world champion, the outcome of the match was obvious well in advance."

The way she said "Your professional obligations are calling you" didn't sound quite Russian. On the other hand, it was the only mistake she made.

"Dubois's valour can only be admired. Despite having played no part in his previous encounters with boxers of ultimately average ability, here, in a match against such a technically flawless opponent as Johnson, Dubois's weaknesses were his undoing."

There's something unnaturally magnetic about her, and perhaps that disharmony in her face might correspond to some sort of psychological anomaly.

"What was so vehemently repeated about Johnson—that he lacked the requisite strength for a knockout blow—was, one may suppose, nothing more than a tactic that has been employed by his manager time and again with great success. It was a publicity stunt *au rebours*, typical of the American sporting press."

What will happen next? I wonder. Rue Octave Feuillet—it isn't far from avenue Henri Martin, unless I'm very much mistaken.

"All Dubois's prior wins can be explained by the fact that none of his opponents has understood the simple necessity to avoid *corps à corps*, or else they have lacked the sufficient technique to execute such a simple plan. Deprived of the ability to initiate *corps à corps*, Dubois immediately lost his main advantage. Johnson grasped this with characteristic presence of mind, and from that moment on Dubois was doomed."

Perhaps some new spiritual journey or departure into the unknown awaits me, as has happened before in my life.

"Let us be utterly frank: despite Dubois's undoubted merits, his claims to the title of world champion were, of course, the result of a misapprehension. He is the honest workhorse of boxing, one of the best that we know; however, he has never had that exceptional and so very rare combination of the various qualities without which a man has no right to one of the foremost places in boxing history. Spanning many years and from among hundreds of boxers, only a few names remain in the memories of the sport's historians, the most recent of these being Carpentier, Dempsey and Tunney. If we are to place Johnson among their ranks, albeit with a degree of uncertainty, then Dubois by comparison could only play the most pitiful of roles. This, however, should in no way detract from his achievements."

Had it not been for that unexpected intonation in her voice, I'd very likely never see her again.

I entered a small café near the printing offices and dashed off the article I had composed in my mind along the way. Then I handed it in to compositing, took a taxi home and lay down to sleep at half past three in the morning. Closing my eyes, I saw before me for the last time the boxers' bare bodies and the illuminated ring, and the unexpected smile of my companion. Finally, I fell asleep to the sound of rain reaching me through the half-open window in my room.

Over the course of the following week, I was awfully busy; I needed money to pay for a multitude of things to which I had scarcely given any thought of late, and it was for this reason that I found myself having to write for a good few hours each day. Since the work more often than not concerned matters with which I was poorly acquainted, I first had to familiarize myself with a certain volume of material.

So it was with the woman whose body had been hacked to pieces: it was necessary to go over the newspaper reports preceding the point in the investigation from which I was picking it up; so it was with the financial scandal; so, too, it was with the disappearance of the eighteen-year-old youth. Yet all my work was in vain: the woman's killer could not be found—this was clear from the outset of the investigation, as soon as it was revealed that her assailant had left no traces. Nor did the bankruptcy of the financial enterprise lead anywhere, and journalists had been instructed not to mention any names. These names belonged to well-known and respected individuals, and so the series of articles on the bank crash was a remarkably short-lived affair, and indeed, after a few days, all mention of it vanished. Everyone knew the sum that had been paid in order to silence the press, but it did not alter the fact that the matter was closed. Lastly, the story surrounding the youth was also no secret to any of us:

it could be explained by his "peculiar morals", as they were termed in official jargon. The young man had simply been whisked away, with his full consent, to the country villa of a renowned artist, also noted for his "peculiar morals", only with a slightly different inclination, whereby his association with the young man constituted a perfect idyll. This artist painted portraits of presidents and ministers, and was closely acquainted with many persons of state, whom he serenely continued to visit. In the reportage of the receptions they held, one could always find the words: "Among those present we noted our renowned artist…" The young man basked in his special (and peculiar) happiness, twenty kilometres outside Paris, while the papers continued to print his photographs, interviews with his relatives, statements given by inspectors from the "social brigade", and so on. Over the course of a single week I wrote fourteen articles about these three events, and this immediately revived my finances. Dubois's manager demanded a rematch, accused the referee of bias and even wrote Dubois's own statement, which explained that he had followed his tactics to the letter, planning to win the fight in the final rounds, and that Johnson's knockout was a patent stroke of luck. Furthermore, the manager persisted in condemning what he called the unacceptable tone adopted by the majority of the reporters on the match, and stressed that he felt ashamed to have read them in the Parisian press. On account of this, a few more articles were published with the official aim of establishing the truth; both the manager and the journalists knew well, however, that the matter had nothing at all to do with the truth, but rather the interests of Dubois's manager, whose fee for subsequent matches would have to be cut following this defeat. It was entirely unavoidable, but he had to do everything to ensure that any reduction would not be too steep.

Throughout all this I felt upbeat yet anxious, just as I would do in my early youth when setting out on a long journey from which I might not have returned. Thoughts of my companion on the night of the Johnson–Dubois match kept coming back to me, and I could tell with absolute certainty of intuition that my next meeting with her was only a matter of time. Inside me a spiritual and physical mechanism had already been set in motion, against which the external circumstances of my life were powerless. I thought about this in a state of constant anxiety, since I knew that I was risking my freedom more than I had done at any other time; to be sure of this it was enough merely to gaze into her eyes, to see her smile and to feel that distinctive, somehow hostile magnetism of hers, which I had sensed on the very first evening of my acquaintance with her. Naturally, I was unaware of what she had felt for me on that February night. Despite having seen her for what was effectively only an hour, in the café after the match, I did sense that her smile and that final intonation in her voice hadn't been accidental, and that it could lead to many other things—perhaps wonderful, perhaps tragic, perhaps at once both tragic and wonderful. Of course, it was always possible that I was mistaken and that my feelings at the time had been just as chance and unreliable as the vague, blurred outlines of the buildings, streets and people seen through that damp, misty veil of rain.

I recalled that she had not asked my name as we were saying goodbye to one another. She would be waiting for me to pay her a visit or to call her, with that placid, almost indifferent self-assurance that seemed completely characteristic of her.

I telephoned her at ten o'clock in the morning, precisely eight days after the match.

"Yes, hello?" said her voice.

"Hello," I said, introducing myself. "I was wondering how you've been."

"Oh, it's you? I'm fine, thank you. I trust you've been well?"

"Yes, it's just that recently there have been so many things that have deprived me of the pleasure of hearing your voice."

"Matters of a personal nature?"

"No, far from it. And they're too boring to recount, especially over the telephone."

"You could perhaps tell me *not* over the telephone."

"For that, I'd require the pleasure of seeing you."

"I'm not in hiding; it can easily be arranged. Where are you dining this evening?"

"I've no idea; I hadn't given it any thought."

"Come to mine around seven, half past seven."

"I'd hate to impose on you."

"If you and I were a little better acquainted, I'd say to you... Do you know what I'd say to you?"

"It isn't difficult to guess."

"In any case, seeing as we aren't sufficiently acquainted, I'll refrain from expressing what I had in mind."

"Your benevolence is appreciated."

"So, I'll expect you this evening?"

"I'll try to be punctual."

At half past seven, I entered the building where she lived; her apartment was located on the first floor. The door opened as soon as I rang. I nearly stepped back in amazement: standing before me was an enormous mulatto, staring silently at me with her eyes wide open. At first I wondered whether I might have been on the wrong floor. However, when I asked if it was possible to see Madame Armstrong, she replied:

"Yes. *Oui, monsieur.*"

She turned and headed towards a second door, evidently leading farther into the apartment; she walked in front of me, spanning the entire breadth of the corridor with her enormous body. She conducted me to the sitting room: on the walls hung a few still lifes of apparently dubious merit; on the floor lay a navy-blue rug, and the furniture was of similarly coloured velvet. For a few seconds I stood examining an elliptical dish, painted yellow, on which lay two sliced and three unsliced oranges—then Yelena Nikolayevna came in. She wore a dress of brown velvet, which suited her very well, as did her hairstyle, which highlighted the tranquil charm of her almost unpainted face. This time, however, her eyes seemed a great deal livelier than they had when I first met her.

THE SPECTRE OF ALEXANDER WOLF

I greeted her and said that the mulatto who had opened the door to me had given me quite a shock. Yelena Nikolayevna smiled.

"She's called Annie," she said. "I call her Little Annie. Do you remember? There was a film a while back."

"Yes, 'Little Annie' is very befitting. Wherever did you find her?"

She explained that Annie began working for her in New York, and now she travelled everywhere with her. She also explained that since Annie had lived in Canada for some time, she spoke French; moreover, she cooked exceedingly well, and I would presently have the opportunity to see for myself. Annie truly was an exceptional cook—I hadn't eaten so well in a long time.

Yelena Nikolayevna enquired about my work over the previous week. I told her about the woman who had been hacked to pieces, about the bankruptcy, about the youth's disappearance and, finally, about the statement made by Dubois's manager in the papers.

"So this is what constitutes working for a newspaper?"

"More or less."

"And it's always like this?"

"More often than not."

"And you think you're suited to it?"

I drank some coffee, smoked and thought about how far removed this conversation was from my feelings and desires. I was silently intoxicated by her presence, and the longer it went on, the more keenly I felt any control over the situation slip away from me, and no amount of effort could overcome these circumstances. I knew that I was behaving properly, that my eyes were bright and that I remained good company—but I knew just as well that this artifice could not fool Yelena Nikolayevna, and she in turn understood that I knew this. The most natural thing to do would have been for me to say to her: "My dear, you aren't mistaken in thinking that this conversation bears no relation at all to what I'm feeling now, or to what you, too, are probably feeling. And you know the words I should be saying right now just as well as I do." Instead of this, however, I said:

"No, of course I'd rather devote myself to literature, but unfortunately it hasn't turned out that way."

"You'd prefer to write lyric tales?"

"Why do you say lyric tales, specifically?"

"It seems as though it ought to be your genre."

"You're telling me this after having met me at the match and after, I hope, you at least rated my prediction regarding its outcome?"

She smiled again.

"Perhaps I'm mistaken. But for some reason it feels as though I've known you for so long, despite this being the second time in my life that I've seen you."

This was her first admission and the first step she took.

"They say that's a very dark omen."

"I'm not afraid," she said with her inexplicably avid smile. I gazed at her grinning mouth, her strong, even teeth, and the dark burgundy hue of her delicately painted lips. I closed my eyes and a stormy, sensual haze washed over me. Despite this, I made an extraordinary effort and managed to remain seated with an outwardly peaceful—or so I thought—expression, although every muscle in my body was so tense that I was in pain.

"You're closing your eyes," said her distant voice. "Perhaps you'd care for a rest after your meal?"

"No, it's just that a certain saying came to mind."

"Which?"

"Something King Solomon said."

"You and I seem to be straying off topic."

This "you and I" was her second move.

"Which saying is it then?"

"It's of note for a certain metaphorical lavishness," I said, "which might now seem somewhat questionable to our ears, in a stylistic sense, of course. But I hope you'll bear in mind that it was written a long time ago."

"God, how you go on! What's the saying?"

"King Solomon said that there were three things he didn't know."

"Which?"

"The path of a serpent on a rock."

"All right."

"The path of an eagle in the sky."

"Fine, as well."

"The path of a woman's heart to the heart of a man."

"No one knows this, it would seem," she said with an unexpectedly thoughtful tone in her voice. "And you think he got it wrong? Why?"

"No, perhaps it's a poor translation. In any case, the last part of the saying doesn't sound right. 'The path of a woman's heart to the heart of a man.' There's something of the grammar book about it."

"I shouldn't delve too far into stylistic analysis. Are you a fan of King Solomon?"

"Not without reservations. Much of what he wrote seems to lack a certain persuasiveness."

It was a gloomy winter's evening, but inside the apartment it was very warm. Yelena Nikolayevna was sitting opposite me, in the armchair, legs crossed; I could see her knees, and every time I looked at them I began to feel suffocated and wretched. I felt that all this—on my part—was beginning to get rather unseemly. I tried to evoke those mental images that I always resorted to for help, as others might resort to mnemonic tricks. Whenever I was gripped violently by a feeling that, for whatever reason, I considered inopportune or, as I did now, premature, I would imagine a great snowy field or the rippling surface of the sea, and it would almost always help me. I tried now to visualize a snowy plain before me—there, where Yelena Nikolayevna was sitting. However, that motionless face with its red lips shone all the more glaringly and starkly through the imaginary whiteness.

Finally I rose, thanked her for her hospitality and prepared to take my leave. When she extended her warm hand to me, however, and I felt her touch against my fingers, I instantly forgot any intention of leaving, just as that night, when saying goodbye to her, I had forgotten my decision not to ask her where she lived and not to seek another meeting with her. I drew her close to me—she winced from the pain I unintentionally inflicted, squeezing her hand too tightly. As I embraced her, I could feel the whole surface of her body. Only later, recalling this episode, did I realize that my sensation at that precise moment must have been illusory: she had been wearing a rather thick velvet dress.

I knew that any other woman in her place would have said only one thing:

"You're mad."

But she did not utter those words. I seemed to be approaching her face as if in some fatal dream. She made not a single movement to resist, but at the last second turned her head to the left, offering up her neck to me. Her dress was fastened at the back by a long row of tightly fitted velvet buttons. When I undid the top two buttons, she said to me with that same calm, though somewhat muted, voice:

"No, not here. Wait a minute. Let me go."

I released her. She went into another room, and I followed her. We had only taken a few steps, but still I had time to reflect on the unexpectedness of it all and the essentially unnatural speed with which all this had happened. Only eight days separated me from the night when I first met her—but this was a vast distance. I knew that my feelings, despite their inherently primitive force—my principal short-coming—usually developed with an arduous sluggishness; these past eight days, however, I had found myself at the mercy of their progression, and I was nevertheless unable to imagine until that final moment how deeply and irreversibly I had been possessed by them. I think that, as with any inexplicable simultaneous attraction of the senses, Yelena Nikolayevna must have felt the same as I did; her feelings were like mine, just as concave glass resembles convex—the same curves, the same double movement. Here was that same incomprehensible impetuosity, which seemed less characteristic of her than it did of me. These thoughts were vague and deceptive, as was everything I felt back then; I remembered them only much later, and in my imagination they assumed a near-crystallized form, which they could not have had during those few brief seconds. In any case, they had seemed of no consequence to me whatsoever at the time.

She let me go on ahead, then shut the door and turned the key in the lock. We found ourselves in a modest room, which I hadn't the time to examine; I noted only a large divan, above which was lit a sconce with a small navy-blue lampshade, a table and, on the table, an ashtray and a telephone. She sat down on the divan; I stopped in front of her for a second, and she managed to say:

"Well, now…"

Through the stormy, sensual murk, I finally glimpsed her body with its tense muscles beneath the shining skin of her arms. She was lying supine, her arms behind her head, without the slightest hint of modesty, gazing at my face with her impossibly serene eyes—it seemed almost incredible. Even when I felt (and not for the first time in my life) that inexplicable synthesis of pure emotion and physical sensation filling not only my entire consciousness, but everything, everything without exception, even the farthest muscles in my body; even then, when she said, "You're hurting me," with so languorous an intonation that

72

it seemed entirely misplaced, betraying neither complaint nor protest; and even then, when she gave a spasmodic shudder—her eyes remained just the same: deathly still. Only in the final moments did her eyes seem distant, like some intonations in her voice.

She could never be called—at least as far as I'm concerned—an excellent lover; her physical reactions were sluggish, and the final seconds of embrace frequently caused her to experience some sort of internal pain; next her eyes would close and her face would involuntarily grimace. However, what set her apart from other women consisted in her making an extreme and exhausting all-out effort, mentally and physically; her irresistible magnetism lay, I think, in the vague sense that close relations with her required some sort of irrevocably destructive effort, and in the infallibility of this presentiment. After experiencing her physical intimacy for the first time, I knew with complete certitude that I would never forget it, and that it might even be the last thing I remembered when I died. I had known this already, and I also knew that no matter what life threw in my path, nothing could save me from the severe and terminal regret that all this would vanish nonetheless, swallowed up whether by death, time or distance, and that the inwardly blinding power of this memory would occupy too great an emotional space in my life and leave no room for other things which may also have been destined for me.

It was already late at night, and Yelena Nikolayevna was unable to hide her fatigue. It felt as though I were in a fever; my eyes were inflamed and I thought I could feel

73

some kind of invisible burning sensation. I left sometime after three o'clock in the morning. It was a cold, starry night. I felt like taking a stroll, and so I walked along the empty streets. Then, for the first time in my life, I found myself in a state of unadulterated happiness, and even the thought that it could be illusory didn't inhibit me. Even now I can remember the buildings I walked past, the taste of the cold winter air, and the gentle breeze at the street corners—these were all linked to the feeling. This sensation of sheer happiness seemed particularly unexpected after having gazed into those motionless eyes for several hours; there had been something humiliating about their expression, precisely because I'd been unable to alter it.

When I awoke the following day, my surroundings and all that to which I was accustomed—the world of people and objects among which my life moved—seemed altered and different, like a forest after the rain.

That night, I parted with her just before daybreak: the next day, by one o'clock in the afternoon, I once again found myself approaching the entrance to her building. I couldn't explain exactly what had changed that night, but it was clear to me that I had never seen rue Octave Feuillet, or avenue Henri Martin, or the building in which she lived in the same light before. The stone walls, the bare trees, the shutters on the building and the steps on the staircase—everything I had known so well and for so long—now acquired a new meaning, which hadn't existed before. It was as if everything were the scenery for the only (and of course finest) play that human imagination could conceive of. It might have been a theatre set. It might also have been a visual overture to a melody (also of course the finest) that was about to begin, a melody that I alone among millions of people could hear, and that was ready to start up the moment that door on the first floor opened to me—a door just like thousands of others, but nevertheless the only one in the world. My wealth of experience, everything I knew, saw and understood, all the tales of betrayal, misfortune and drama, and the tragic infidelity of everything in existence, were powerless to interrupt this; it appeared that what I had so vainly waited for my entire life was finally happening, and that no man other than I would be able to understand this, for the sole reason that no one had lived as I had, and no one knew the combination of things that epitomized my existence. It seemed that if the story of my life were to have lacked a single detail, this feeling of happiness and my understanding of it could never have been so complete. Everything felt at once completely unquestionable, yet so incredible. As I walked along avenue Victor Hugo, it suddenly occurred to me that none of this could be real, and I began to experience a sort of emotional vertigo—as though all this were a page from a children's book about vanishing acts.

Annie told me that *madame* would be out presently and conducted me into the dining room. The modest table was already laid for two, complete with wine glasses—in one of them a thin shaft of light played, as if filling it with an invisible, spectral liquid; I remembered then that the weather was wintry but sunny. I sat down in an armchair and lit a cigarette. I became conscious that I was smoking only when the ash, falling from the cigarette, burned my hand and landed on my sleeve.

Yelena Nikolayevna came into the room a few seconds before Annie began serving breakfast. She had just taken a bath and hadn't bothered to dress. She was wearing a dressing gown; her hair was combed back, and this imparted a particular clarity to her features, while simultaneously affording her an air of mental and physical comfort, both pleasant and unexpected. She asked me with ironic tenderness in her voice whether I had slept well and whether I had any appetite. Looking straight at her, I replied in the affirmative. She too had changed, as with everything else I saw around me; the expression of estrangement that I had felt until now had vanished from her face. As she leant over the table I spotted the large birthmark under her right collarbone; a warm wave of gratitude and tenderness towards her flowed over me, and then I caught her still gaze.

"What are you thinking about?" I asked.

"About how you and I have known each other for such a short period of time, and yet I don't think I've ever known anyone who has been closer to me than you are now."

Then she added:

"I shan't always say such things, so don't get used to it."

She poured the wine. It was an unusual, fragrant, strong wine, and however little I might know about wines even I could not fail to notice that it was, very probably, a particularly fine one. Then she asked:

"What shall we drink to?"

"To not getting used to it," I said.

She nodded indulgently, and we drank in silence. The words had sounded almost solemn, like those said perhaps once in a lifetime, when going off to war or leaving for good—despite this being essentially a breakfast like any other, with a woman whom I had met a week ago and who the previous night had become my lover. And just as she was neither the first nor the only one in my life, so too I was neither her first nor her only lover.

After breakfast, we sat together for a long time over coffee. Wisps of cigarette smoke curled and vanished in the sunlight that came beating through the window. She was still wearing her dressing gown, and when I mentioned this to her, she answered with a smile:

"I'm not expecting anyone; I have no one to dress for. As far as you're concerned, I'd even wager that you'd prefer me without the dressing gown, and just imagine what would happen then. No, wait," she said, seeing me move as though to get up from my armchair. "Wait. I'm here, I'm not going anywhere, and I have no desire to leave you. I just wanted to chat with you. Tell me what your life was like before now. Whom did you love and what made you happy?"

"I hardly know where to begin," I said. "It's all so complicated, long and contradictory. When I wake up every morning, I think to myself, Today my life will begin in earnest. I'll feel as though I'm not much older than sixteen again, and that man who has known so much tragedy and sadness, he who fell asleep in my bed the previous night, will seem alien and distant, and I'll comprehend neither his inner weariness nor his frustration. Then, as I go to sleep every night, I feel as though I've lived a long life, and yet all I've taken from it is the loathing and burden of lingering years. And so the day passes. As it nears its end, the poison of inner weariness pierces me deeper still. But this, of course, isn't the story of my life. What I'm telling you is how I used to feel, until that evening when you, by some stroke of good fortune, couldn't get a ticket for the match."

"You're relatively young and, as far as I can see, the picture of health," she said. "And whatever you say, I don't believe in your inner weariness. If you could only take the time to look at yourself, you'd understand why your words of fatigue sound so unconvincing."

"I never said that I felt this inner weariness with regard to you. And when I see you…"

"It's as though it were morning?"

"It's as though it were morning."

"Be that as it may, we're veering away from the main issue here," she said. "Where were you born, where did you grow up, where did you go and why did you leave? And what is your surname, seeing as I still only know your Christian name? Where did you study, or didn't you study at all?"

"Yes, I studied," I said. "Probably to no avail, but I studied for a long time, and quite a variety of subjects."

I began telling her about myself. Never before had my own fate seemed as clear to me as it did now. Among my memories, I encountered many things I had failed to spot before, some of them almost lyrical; I was struck by the vague sensation (without having to break my narrative) that, were it not for Yelena Nikolayevna, I would probably never have been able to uncover the potency and freshness of these recollections that had appeared so suddenly. Perhaps they didn't even exist beyond the very presence and thought of this woman sitting next to me in her dressing gown, with her hair smoothly brushed and the far-off gaze of eyes sunk in thought.

"You'll have to forgive me if my story doesn't conform to any strict chronological order," I said.

She nodded. I told her of many things that day: of war, Russia, travels, my childhood. An assortment of people I had once known appeared to me: teachers, officers, soldiers, officials, classmates—whole countries passed before my eyes. My memory evoked images of subtropical landscapes, regular patches of brown earth, narrow white roads, and the creak of a poor wooden cart that could be heard from afar in the hot still air; the sad eyes of a small, half-starved cow, harnessed alongside a donkey to a plough, which a Greek peasant in a dark-grey burnous and a white felt hat was using to till the hard earth; I recalled also that in Turkey distance is measured by time—it isn't however many kilo-metres to such-and-such a place, but rather however many hours on foot; I recalled the icy winds of central Russia and the springy crunch of snow underfoot, then the seas, the rivers, the wild ducks on the Danube and the steamships and trains—everything through which the inexplicable movements of my life had passed. Then I returned once more to the war and to those thousands of bodies that I had seen—and suddenly I recalled the speech my Russian teacher had given during his final address to us:

"You are beginning to live. Taking part in what is called the struggle for life lies ahead of you. Roughly speaking, there are three types: the struggle for victory, the struggle for annihilation, and the struggle for consensus. You are all young and full of vigour, and so, naturally, you are drawn to the first type. But always remember that the most humane and most advantageous is the struggle for consensus. If you make of this a principle throughout your life, it will mean that the culture we have tried to bestow on you will not have been for nothing, that you have become true citizens of the world, and, consequently, we shall not have lived in this world in vain. Because, if it be otherwise, it will mean that we have merely wasted our time. We are old, we have no more strength to build a new life. We have one hope left, and that is you."

"I think he was right," I said. "Unfortunately, however, we didn't always have the occasion to choose the type of struggle we thought best."

"Do you have fond memories of your teachers?"

She and I were sitting on the divan. I had my right arm around her, and I could feel the warmth of her body through the towel dressing gown.

"No, not of all of them. Far from it," I said, smiling. I was thinking of one of the priests who taught us Scripture in the upper forms; he was a tall, absent-minded man, who wore a lilac silk cassock. His voice betrayed an inherent boredom:

"There is much evidence of God's existence. There is juridical evidence, there is logical evidence and there is philosophical evidence."

Then he paused for a moment and added:

"There is even mathematical evidence, but I've forgotten it."

"Where did you go to university? In Paris?"

"Yes, but it wasn't quite so simple."

I told her how I had needed to collect a piece of paper from the former Russian consul, which only he could issue to me and which replaced my birth certificate. He was a rather short, irate old man with an enormous grey beard, who said to me:

"I shan't give you anything of the sort. Why, I don't know you from Adam. You might be a professional crook for all I know, maybe even a murderer or some bandit. This is the first time I've ever seen you in my life. Whom do you know in Paris?"

"No one," I said. "A handful of my former classmates are here, but they're all in the same position as I am; none of them is known to you personally, and there is nothing to stop you supposing that each of them, too, is a professional crook or murderer and also my accomplice."

"What do you need this piece of paper for?"

"I'd like to matriculate at university."

"You? University?"

"Yes, if you'll permit me to have this piece of paper."

"For that, my dear fellow, you need to have a secondary education."

"I have a leaving certificate."

"And you must know French."

"I do."

"Where on earth did you have the occasion to study?"

"Back home, in Russia."

"Lord knows," he said doubtfully. "Perhaps you aren't a bandit after all. I make no categorical assertion either way; I haven't the factual information with which to do so. Do show me your certificate."

He glanced over it, then suddenly asked:

"Why only average marks in algebra and trigonometry, eh?"

"I never did have any aptitude for the so-called exact sciences."

"All right, I'll give you the piece of paper. But see here, it's on your own responsibility."

"Very well," I said. "If I'm arrested and thrown in jail, I promise not to allude to you."

I laughed, remembering the old fellow, and she laughed with me; I could feel her whole body vibrating through the surface of my hand. She then stood up, threw me what seemed to be a look of reproach and drew the blinds; a dark grey filled the room. In the quiet that descended, I could hear music coming from the apartment above, where someone was playing the piano very slowly and deliberately, creating the impression that great drops of sound were falling one after the other into molten glass.

*

It was clear to me that the principal distinguishing feature of my relationship with Yelena Nikolayevna was an absence of any single moment during which my senses were not in a heightened state. If not a desire for her intimacy, it was tenderness; if not tenderness, it was a whole succession of other feelings or emotional states, to define which I knew neither the words, nor the means by which to find these words. In any case, I was indebted to her existence for the discovery of a world that I had previously not known. I hadn't imagined what physical intimacy with a woman could mean, and I found it strange to think that all this could be compared with my previous affairs. I knew that each love was essentially unique, but this was a very simplistic and inexact assertion. Under any degree of scrutiny, similarities can always be found; what is unique consists in the certain chance nuances of certain chance intonations. This time it was different—unlike anything that had gone before it—and among all my emotional experience I could find nothing to remind me of my current situation. I thought that after the destructive exertions of this love I would have no strength left for any other feeling, and that, for me, nothing would ever compare with this unendurable memory. Wherever I was and whatever I was doing, all I had to do was think for a few seconds, and before me would appear her face, with those distant eyes, and that smile of hers that contained such naive shamelessness, as if she were standing there completely naked. And yet, despite the strength of my physical attraction to her, it failed to resemble the wildest passion, because a streak of icy purity and some strange, uncharacteristic disinterestedness always seemed to pervade it. I hadn't known myself to be capable of such feelings, although I suppose they were feasible only relative to her—and therein ended her true uniqueness and wonder for me.

As always, whenever confronted by something new in life, I find myself unable to tell what has summoned it out of non-existence. I could find no answer in my attempts to learn what exactly had imbued Yelena Nikolayevna with that irresistible magnetism of hers. I had known women more beautiful than she, I had heard voices more melodious than hers, but her placid face and humiliating, calm eyes apparently held the power to create a rather painful impression on me. She was practically devoid of that warmth of feeling I so valued; there was almost no tenderness in her, or, more accurately, it surfaced only rarely and always as if unintentionally. She had no "charm"; the notion was quite unsuited to her. Yet, she was, as far as I was concerned, unique and wonderful, and nothing could alter this.

She could never have been called secretive. However, a lengthy acquaintance or genuine intimacy was first required to know what her life had entailed before then, what she liked, what she did not like, what interested her, and what she valued in the people she encountered. It was a long time before she revealed any opinions that could shed light on her character, even though I talked with her on the most diverse of topics; she would usually listen in silence or respond monosyllabically. Over the course of many weeks I learnt little more about her than I had done in those first few days. Yet she had no reason to hide anything from me;

it was simply the remnants of her intrinsic sense of reserve, which could only seem strange to me. Whenever I asked about anything, she would be disinclined to answer, and this would never fail to surprise me. She would remark:

"Isn't it all the same to you?"

Or:

"Of what possible interest could that be?"

But I was interested in everything about her. I wanted to find out what had happened in her life before we met.

One of her traits was a peculiar inner sluggishness that did not tally with the swiftness and precision of her movement in general: her quick step, her impeccable, instantaneous physical reflexes. Only amid what constituted an indefinable union of the spiritual and the physical—love, for example—was the ordinarily faultless harmony of her body broken, and, for her, there was always something almost excruciating about this chance dissonance. That impression of a strange, almost anatomical, disharmony that I noted on the evening of our first meeting (that is to say, the combination of her high, well-shaped forehead and that avid smile) was no coincidence. There was an undoubted discordancy between the composition of her body and the progress of her inner life, which lagged slowly behind this robust being. Had it been possible to separate these and forget about this, she would have been completely happy. Loving her demanded constant creative effort. She never did anything for the sake of creating some sort of impression; she never gave any thought to the effect her words had. She existed independently of her surroundings, and her feelings towards others were dictated either by some physical attraction, as real as the desire to sleep or eat, or else by some urge, similar to that of the majority of people, but different in that under no circumstances would she act other than how she wanted. The wishes of others came into play only while they coincided with her own. Almost since the very first days of our acquaintance, I had been astounded by her incautious nature, her indifference to what others might think of what she was saying. Yet, with that cold and obstinate love of hers, she loved dangerous and powerful emotions.

Such was her nature—to alter this, I think, would have been exceedingly difficult. Nevertheless, as time went on I began to notice some signs of human warmth in her; little by little she was thawing. I questioned her at length about everything, but she would reply comparatively rarely—and tersely, at that. She told me that she grew up in Siberia, in the back of beyond, where she had lived until the age of fifteen. The first city she ever saw was Murmansk. She was an only child, and her parents had died at sea: during the voyage from Russia to Sweden, their ship had struck a floating mine. She was seventeen at the time and living in Murmansk. Soon after this, she married an American engineer, the very same man of whose sudden death she had been informed via telegram a year ago in London. She explained to me that she had liked him because he had a streak of grey in his hair, and also because he was a deft skier and ice skater, and had many fascinating things to say about America. They left Russia together; it was around the time when, at the other end of that enormous country, amid the exhausting senselessness of the Civil War, I had roamed the scorching southern steppes with their burnt grass, under the high sun. She spoke of a round-the-world voyage: how the transatlantic liner she was travelling aboard had navigated the Bosporus by night, and then the Sea of Marmara and the Aegean Sea; how hot it had been, and how she had danced the foxtrot. I remembered those nights and their particular dark, sultry heat, and how I had sat for hours atop the high bank of the Dardanelles, looking out through the stifling darkness at the lights of these enormous ships passing by so near to me that I could hear the music of their orchestras and see the slowly retreating rows of portholes as the ships sailed off, blending into at first a glittering, then fading, and then finally dim speck of light. Perhaps I might have seen her ship, watching it in that same avid, blind state of tension in which I found myself during all those initial years of my life abroad.

For many years she had led an interesting life, full of unexpected events, journeys, encounters and a few of what she termed "inescapable" love affairs. She had been to Austria, Switzerland, Italy, France and America, and in each of these countries she had spent a considerable period of time. She arrived in England for the first time two and a half years prior to this.

"After that, it was all plain sailing," she said.

"Plain sailing… meaning Paris, rue Octave Feuillet, the Johnson–Dubois match, and so on? By the way, what were you banking on, turning up without a ticket? Ticket touts?"

"Ticket touts—or luck. As you can see, I wasn't wrong to do so."

"Have the results of the match exceeded your expectations?"

"In certain respects, yes."

The more I learnt, the more I grew used to the unnatural divide between the inner life and physical life that was so characteristic of her. This divide had probably always existed within her, but now there was something almost unhealthy about it, and numerous times the thought struck me that the current period in her life must have been preceded by some sort of shock, of which I knew nothing and which she, in turn, avoided mentioning. Life with her consisted of two sharply contrasting love affairs: a sensual intimacy, in which everything was, on the whole, natural, and a spiritual affinity, infinitely slower, more complex and which may not have been there at all. An initial assessment of what was happening—by any man who was to become her lover— would inevitably prove erroneous, and these errors would be all the more inescapable precisely because they would be so completely natural. Time and again I imagined the chain of mistakes. The first error would consist of the idea that any development in events could depend on the man. In fact, the decision would always stem from her, and not only the decision, but even that first subtle move marking the beginning of the affair, often encompassing everything that is to follow. However, this particularity of hers, of course, was in no way exceptional: as I had always known, in most cases the beginning and denouement of any affair depends entirely on the woman. The second mistake would consist in the affair being considered in some way definitive. In reality, it meant nothing, or almost nothing, and could be halted at any given moment without the slightest explanation or any chance of reviving it whatsoever. The third and gravest mistake was that, if one were to judge by appearances, one might have thought the affair long already to have been a fait accompli, whereas, in fact, the real affair would begin only after the passage of much time and in the case of some rare and happy coincidence. I searched long and hard for a comparison that could exemplify this, but still I couldn't find one: it could have been said to resemble the touch of cold lips, which warm slowly and only then regain their lost, burning delight—or else they might never regain it, leaving instead the memory of icy discontent and vain regret for what could have been and never was. Yet the most unchanging aspect of relations with her was the unconscious, inescapable strain on all one's inner strength, without which an intimacy with her could be only aleatory and episodic. This in no way resulted from her unduly exacting nature, but rather came about of itself and even, it would seem, apart from her own wishes. It was just so, at any rate, and apparently could not have been otherwise. Moreover, it posed no difficulty, judging by a few of her admissions, to draw the conclusion that everyone who knew her intimately probably agreed to a greater or lesser extent.

Much later, recalling our first meeting and how everything had begun, I found it easier to reconstruct events by closing my eyes and hypothetically omitting the content of our initial conversation in the café, our parting under the rain, and generally those things whose substance can fit into a cohesive narrative. More keenly than ever before in my life I sensed that all this came down to some blind, obscure movement, to a sequence of visual and aural impressions, accompanied by an unconscious, simultaneous muscular gravity that was developing uncontrollably. Johnson's torso, Dubois on the canvas, the touch of my fingers on her hand when I helped her into the taxi, this whole silent melody of skin and muscles, the counter jolt from her body, of which even she may have been unaware—this was of the greatest importance, and this predetermined what was to come. What did she know about me on that misty February evening, and why had she waited a whole week for my call? When she smiled at me for the first time with that avid smile of hers, I knew then that she would belong to me. However, she knew this even earlier than I did. This was heralded, of course, by the downfall of an abstract world that scorned any primitive and purely physical understanding, a world where a peculiar philosophy of life built upon the prior rejection of the pre-eminence of materialistic factors was incomparably more important than any sensual reactions, a world that vanished instantaneously that evening in this silent muscular action. When I mentioned this once to Yelena Nikolayevna, she replied with a smile:

"Perhaps it's because we'd still make do even without any philosophy, whereas humanity would be threatened by extinction, in one form or another, if it weren't for the other thing you mention."

I often felt uncomfortable in her presence, especially at first. I very quickly grew convinced that her reactions bore no similarity to those of the majority of other women. To make her laugh, for example, one couldn't employ the same techniques that made others laugh; to elicit any feeling in her, one had to seek out an innovative new route, unlike any ordinary one. I had to expend much time and effort fine-tuning myself to the emotional world in which my intimacy with her took place. At last, however, I was leading a real life that was not half composed (as it had been until now) of memories, regrets, forebodings and vague expectations.

Yelena Nikolayevna and I often went on long walks around Paris. She knew Paris poorly and superficially. I showed her the real city, not the one featured in the illustrated newspapers or the one that remained so inalterable in the imaginations of tourists who came here for a fortnight each year; I showed her the impoverished working-class districts, the backstreets far away from the centre, buildings on the city outskirts, a few of the quays, boulevard de Sébastopol at four o'clock in the morning. I remember how she gazed at rue Saint-Louis-en-l'Île with such wonderment. It was truly difficult to imagine how in this city, with its magnificent avenues radiating off from place de l'Étoile, there could be such a narrow, dark passageway between two rows of ancient buildings, steeped in age-old must, against which all civilization was powerless. It was already late spring. After the long, steadfast cold of winter, with all its gloomy scenery, we opened our eyes to a different Paris: the limpid nights, the distant red glow over Montmartre, and the solid rows of chestnut trees lining boulevard Arago, where we somehow kept ending up for a period. I walked with my arm around her waist, and, without the slightest hint of protest, she said to me in a lazy, calm voice:

"My dear, you're behaving like a complete *apache*."

Before returning home, we would occasionally stop off at an all-night café or a bar, and she would be amazed that I, no matter in which district we found ourselves, would always know the face of every waiter and every woman sitting at the bar, waiting for the next client. Yelena Nikolayevna drank only spirits; she was unusually resilient to the effects of alcohol, a fact explained, I think, by prolonged training and stays in Anglo-Saxon countries. Only having drunk a significant volume of alcohol would she begin to act differently than usual, and she would, without fail, be drawn to places where she ought not to have gone. "Let's go to the Bastille, to a *bal musette*; I want to watch the *gens du milieu*. Let's go to rue Blondel, to that notorious brothel."—"Lenochka, it's such a bore."—"Well then, where do the queers get together around here? You must know. What sort of journalist are you? Let's go, I beg you. I do so love the queers."—"Say we go and somebody takes a knife to me. What would you do then?"—"There's no need to cast yourself in such a falsely heroic light: no one's going to hurt you. That would be like something from a bad novel." Sometimes she would come up with totally wild ideas. I remember how she once asked me where it was possible to buy sweets at night. Without the slightest inkling of her true intentions, I told her. We were in a taxi, and so she ordered the driver to go to the shop; she came out, her arms laden with bags of sweets.

"What are you going to do with all this?"

"My dear," she said in a tender voice, entirely unlike her normal one and from which I could discern that she was quite drunk—this had not been apparent until now. "I'll kiss you, I'll do whatever you want, only just grant me my one little request."

"Oh, here it comes," I said, thinking aloud.

"But it's this small," she continued, pointing to the nail on her little finger. "You must know—I'm sure you do—the districts where I can find the little ten- to fifteen-year-old prostitutes."

"No, I haven't the faintest idea."

"Do you want me to ask the driver? You'll look a complete fool."

"But what do you want these girls for?"

"I want to hand out the sweets, you see. It'll be nice for them."

Only with great effort did I manage to dissuade her from executing this plan. Sometimes, however, she insisted so much that I had no choice other than to restrain her by force or give in. Thus we went almost anywhere she wanted, but I noticed that none of these places, in fact, held much interest for her. She was simply giving free rein to some sudden caprice of hers, but as soon as it became easily achieved, it lost a significant portion of its allure for her. She was ready to do anything for the sake of powerful sensations. But there were none to be had. There were just pimps in light-grey caps, displaying a deferential fear towards the policemen guarding the entrance to the *bal musette*, plump naked women with drooping bodies and deadly animal stupidity in their eyes, and made-up youths with unsteady gaits and an inexplicable hint of spiritual syphilis on their faces. And she said:

"You're right, it is boring."

She loved going for a spin in a motor car. When she asked me one day to hire a car without a driver, we journeyed out of town and I credulously let her take the wheel; she drove at breakneck speed, and I was not wholly convinced that we would ever return from this jaunt without first ending up in hospital. She was an exceptionally able driver, but whenever we came to a turn or a crossroads I still found myself wanting to close my eyes and forget where I was. After miraculously escaping our third collision, I finally said to her:

"We could have crashed three times already."

Without reducing speed, she took her left hand from the steering wheel, raised her index finger and replied:

"Once."

"How so?"

"Because after the first crash we couldn't have driven any farther; the opportunity for further crashes wouldn't have presented itself."

On the way back, however, I categorically refused to allow her behind the wheel. While we were driving, she said to me:

"I can't understand you. You drive just as quickly as I

do. What are you afraid of? Do you think you're a better driver than I am?"

"No," I said, "I'm not so sure about that. But I do know the road; I know which crossroads are dangerous and which aren't, whereas you're driving blind."

She looked at me with a strange expression in her eyes and said:

"Blind? I think it's all the more interesting that way. Everything is, generally."

It was around this time that I received a commission to write a series of articles on literature, allowing me at long last to rid myself of all the erratic, uninteresting jobs. One day, Yelena Nikolayevna paid me a visit—it was her first and came without any forewarning, and so, after the unexpected ring, I was very surprised to see her upon opening the door.

"Hello," she said, looking round the room where I was working. "I wanted to catch you unawares and, perhaps, in another woman's embrace."

She stood by the bookshelves, rapidly extracting one volume after the next and then setting them back in their place. Suddenly her gaze fell on me; her eyes bore a shade of expression that I had never before seen in them.

"What's the matter?"

"Nothing. One of your books just caught my interest. I've always wanted to read it, but I could never find it anywhere."

"Which one?"

"*The Golden Ass*," she said hastily. "May I borrow it?"

It surprised me that this book could have created such an impression on her.

"Of course," I said, "but it's nothing earth-shattering."

"My husband gave me a copy on our honeymoon; I began reading it, but accidentally dropped it into the sea. Later I asked for another copy everywhere, but I couldn't find one. True, what I had was an English translation, whereas this one is in Russian... Anyway, what are you working on at the moment?"

I showed her what I was writing; she asked whether she might help me.

"Yes, of course, but I'm afraid you might find it a bore trawling through books and copying out quotes."

"No, on the contrary, I'd find it interesting."

She insisted so much that I consented. Her task consisted in copying and translating the passages I underlined, which were to be included in the article as illustrations of whatever literary point I was developing. She did this so quickly and with such ease that it seemed almost second nature to her. Moreover, she displayed a degree of learning that I would never have suspected of her: English literature was certainly her forte.

"Where did this come from?" I asked. "You said it had all been travelling and love affairs—where did you find the time for all this reading?"

"If writing articles about political villains, people who punch each other in the face and women who are cut into pieces didn't stop you, then why should my love affairs prevent me from reading books? They don't take long: one-two and you're done."

Glancing up from the book in her hands, she gazed at me with mocking eyes.

She began to visit me almost every day. Once I took her in my arms, but she pushed me aside, saying:

"We can kiss this evening: right now it's time for work."

She brought such seriousness to it all that it would sometimes cause me to laugh inadvertently. However, I could not but value her help; my work was going twice as quickly. Occasionally she would wake me up with her arrival in the morning; this was due to a long-standing force of habit, whereby I would go to bed late at night and rise late the following day. By the end of May, the weather had already turned hot. I would work with her by day, and we would dine together in the evening; later on, we would go out, and I would accompany her home afterwards, usually staying with her while she performed her evening toilet. When she came out of the bathroom with a white face and pale lips (the lipstick removed), I would take off her dressing gown, tuck her into bed and ask:

"Now, do you need a lullaby?"

Leaving her in the dead of night, I would step out into the street and set off homeward. Life began to seem incredible to me; I still could not accustom myself to the idea that, at last, my life lacked any tragedy, that I was doing work that interested me, that there was a woman I loved as I had never loved anyone before—she was neither mad nor hysterical, and I did not have to be on guard every moment, waiting for an outburst of unexpected passion, an attack of incomprehensible malice, or those pointless, uncontrollable tears. Everything that my existence had comprised until now—regrets, dissatisfaction and a sense of the manifest futility of everything I did—began to seem very distant and alien to me, as though I were thinking of something that had taken place long ago. Among these disappearing objects and fading recollections was the memory of Alexander Wolf and his story "The Adventure in the Steppe". His book stood, as before, on my shelf, but much time had passed since I last opened it.

Entering Yelena Nikolayevna's apartment one day (I had my own key), I was greeted by her singing. I paused. She was humming some Spanish love song. It was one of those tunes that could have been composed only in the south, one whose origins could not be conceived of without sunlight. In some inscrutable way the melody contained light, just as others might contain snow, or impart a sense of the night. When I entered the room she smiled and said to me:

"The funny thing is that I never suspected for a moment that I'd actually remember this song. I heard it around four years ago at a concert, then once later on a gramophone—and suddenly it's all come back to me."

"Perhaps, really," I said, believing I was responding to her thought, "everything isn't quite so tragic after all, and everything that's positive is not always and necessarily illusory."

"You're always so warm and fuzzy," she said without any reference to the start of the conversation, "and, when you're not being sarcastic, your thoughts are warm and fuzzy, too. Your gift for thinking interferes with you: without it, of course, you'd be happy."

I was utterly rapt in my earlier desire to find out what had happened to her before her arrival in Paris. What was it exactly? Which feeling had become so lastingly frozen in her eyes? And what was the source of this inner coldness in her? I knew from long experience, however, that the charm and appeal of a woman exists for me only so long as there remains something uncertain about her—some unknown dimension that affords me the possibility (or the illusion) of reconstructing an image of her again and again, imagining her as I would like her to be and, probably, not as she is in reality. It never reached the stage whereby I would prefer a lie or a falsehood to the too simple truth; however, a thoroughgoing knowledge carried with it a certain danger: you did not want to return to this, much as to a book, previously read and understood. And yet, the desire to know was always inseparable from the emotion, and no amount of reasoning could alter this. Without this palpable psychological danger, life would probably have seemed too dull to me. I was convinced that some shadow was cast over a certain period in Yelena Nikolayevna's life, and I wanted to know whose eyes had found their permanent reflection in hers, whose chill had penetrated her body so deeply—more importantly, how and why this had happened.

However strong my desire was to find out, I didn't rush; I hoped that I would still have sufficient time. I first sensed the possibility of Yelena Nikolayevna's emotional trust in me when one day, sitting next to me on the divan, she suddenly placed her hands on my shoulder in an uncertain and quite unfamiliar move. This gesture, entirely atypical of her, was more revealing than any words could be. I watched her face; her eyes could not keep up with her body and still retained their expression of calmness. I perceived that she was no longer the woman she had been only a little while ago. Perhaps she would never be that woman again. Sometimes, in telling me a few insignificant details from one or another period in her life, she would say to me "my lover at the time" or "he was one of my lovers". Each time, hearing these words on her lips and in relation to her, I would experience an unpleasant sensation, despite knowing that it could not be otherwise and that it was impossible to exclude even a single event from her life without her ceasing to exist for me thereafter, because I would never have met her had she had a single lover more or fewer. Besides, she would utter the word in such a tone, as if she were talking about some unimportant, ephemeral servant.

Time and again I observed (with unfailing wonderment) that women in general were remarkably frank with me and particularly keen to tell me their life stories. I'd heard a multitude of confessions, occasionally even those of a nature that made me feel uncomfortable. Seemingly most inexplicable was that in fact I had very little to do with the majority of these women; I was linked to them through mere acquaintance. Many times I asked myself the question: what, strictly speaking, could account for such outpourings, entirely unwarranted from any perspective?

Since it ultimately interested me very little, however, I never spent too much time considering the reasons behind it. I knew only that women were frank with me, and this was more than sufficient, because from time to time it landed me in awkward situations. Yelena Nikolayevna was, in this sense, exceptional. True, a few times she had been capable of saying "my former lover" or "my lover at the time", all in the same tone of voice with which she might say "my laundress" or "my cook", but that was where it ended. Very rarely would she have these brief moments of candour: she would tell me something, and then all of a sudden she would be cruel to me, with her crudeness of expression and references to certain too realistic details. I pitied her. However, what she had hitherto never spoken of—under any circumstances—was her inner life.

I was sitting next to her one evening; through the half-drawn curtains came a dull glow from the round street lamps. Above the divan the sconce was lit. I stood up and walked over to the window. The sky was starry and clear.

"Sometimes I feel sorry for you," I said. "I get the impression that you've been deceived over and over again, and every time you've said something that might have been better left unsaid you've subsequently had to repent of it. I'm afraid that among your admirers there will have been those who cannot be called gentlemen—and now it's a case of once bitten, twice shy."

I turned around. She said nothing; her face wore a distant, vacant expression.

"Or perhaps," I continued, "you have a sort of emotional

pneumothorax. But what doctor would have had the cruelty to do that."

"Two years ago in London," she said in her calm, languid voice, "I met a man."

Some almost imperceptible intonation of hers forced me to put up my guard at once. I remained standing by the window. I thought that if I were to go up to her or sit in the armchair next to the divan, or even if I were to take a few steps about the room, my initial movement would suddenly disturb her frame of mind, and I would never find out what she had wanted to tell me. I dared not even turn my head. Thus, in this tense state of immobility, I began listening to her tale. Now she spoke with full and unguarded candour: what I had waited for so long and so patiently was finally happening.

It began with a party held by an acquaintance of hers. The host was a man of fifty; his wife was twenty years his junior.

I wanted to ask what significance the detail about the respective ages of the hosts held for later events, but I held my peace.

The rather substantial meal was followed by some improvised entertainment. One of the guests sang fairly well, another read poetry, and one lady danced very pleasingly. The last to perform was a tall man who played some pieces by Scriabin on the piano. The music left a tremendously painful impression on Yelena Nikolayevna, which she unwittingly associated with the player. When, in the middle of the evening, he invited her to dance, it took a great effort from her not to refuse him. However, he danced wonderfully and proved, according to her, to be the most engaging dance partner she had ever come across. His face was pale, and his eyes glittered. What he said was clever and true, and his words somehow always fell in time with the music that accompanied their dancing. This man was a friend of the host's and the lover of his wife: Yelena Nikolayevna saw the intent look of the hostess's dark-blue eyes, never leaving him for a second as they danced.

They spoke of America, Hollywood, Italy and Paris; he had a thorough knowledge of them all, as though he had lived everywhere for many years. He had read all the latest books—in this he was exceptionally erudite; he knew music well, yet understood nothing of painting. When the evening reached its end and he came up to her to take his leave, she noticed for the first time, with surprise, that he was not overly young; in these few minutes it seemed as if there had been some strange transformation in his face. However, she recalled this impression only much later.

A week passed. He telephoned, and she met him in a restaurant where they dined. He was exactly as he had been on the evening of their first meeting. A band of Hungarian Gypsies was playing; there was the wailing sound of violins and their usual, painfully seductive stretching of the melody, which would suddenly break off in favour of a brisk rhythm, like an aural depiction of horses galloping along some vast imaginary plain. He listened attentively and then said:

"In Europe there's only one country where it's truly possible to understand what space means—that's Russia.

103

But perhaps you don't care for geography, least of all in a restaurant. Everything that happens is truly miraculous, don't you think?"

"I've heard those exact words said so many times that they've lost all standing with me."

"Nevertheless, it's just so, and your poor friends were right."

"Sometimes there's nothing duller than being right."

"Naturally. But if you were to trouble yourself to imagine the chain of events in the life of a single human being, you'd have to agree that it's almost always miraculous."

"More often than not they're simply uninteresting. And in many cases it's unclear precisely why a person has lived so pointlessly and unnecessarily."

"I'll tell you a story," he said. "The life of a poor Jewish boy from Poland, who was born into a grocer's family, but dreamt of being a tailor. He fought in the war, was captured, fought again, was wounded, and after many trials he wound up in England, where he succeeded in becoming a tailor, as he had always hoped he would. He dreamt of this in the sodden trenches, amid the roar of gunfire, in hospital and in captivity. After receiving his first order, he fell ill with pneumonia and died ten days later. Just think, what an exceptional chain of events, what a magnificent end!"

"And you see the manifestation of some higher meaning in all this?"

His face took on a serious air; his sparkling eyes bore into her.

"Surely it's obvious to you? It was a race towards death. He dreamt of becoming a tailor, as others dream of riches or glory. Fate seemingly preserved him so that he could achieve this aim. He wasn't killed on the front, he didn't perish in captivity, and he didn't die of gangrene or blood poisoning in hospital. Finally, when his dream comes true, it turns out that its very realization heralds his own death, towards which he's been striving all this time. Every life becomes clear—that is to say, its path, its twists and turns—only in its final moments. Do you know the Persian legend about the gardener and Death?"

"No."

"A gardener comes to the Shah one day, in extreme agitation, and says to him: 'Lend me your swiftest steed; I needs must go as far as I can, to Isfahan. Just now, while working in the garden, I saw my own death.' The Shah gives him a horse, and the gardener gallops off to Isfahan. The Shah goes into the garden; Death is standing there. The Shah says to Death: 'Why did you frighten my gardener, appearing before him like that?' Death answers the Shah: 'I didn't mean to. Indeed I was surprised to see your gardener here, for in my book it's written that I'm to meet him this evening, far away, in Isfahan.'"

Then he added:

"I know many instances where the meaning of such a path is particularly clear. I told you about the tailor. Here's another example for you: a Russian officer, a participant in the Great War, and later the Civil War in Russia. He spent six years on the front line. Nearly all his comrades

105

perished. He was wounded a few times and once crawled four kilometres under fire, with two bullets in his body. Many times nothing short of a miracle saved him from death. Still, he remained alive. Then the war ended, and he came to peaceful Greece, where nothing seemed able to threaten him. The day after his arrival, he was taking an evening stroll around the outskirts of a small Asiatic village; he fell into a well and drowned. Just think then whether it was worth making such a terrific effort to crawl all that distance under fire, passing out from weakness. Was it worth wasting such unwavering bravery and hero- ism only to drown one night in a well, having left all that danger behind?"

"So you think the idea behind everything in existence can be reduced to this deadly fatalism?"

"It isn't fatalism, it's the direction of life. It's the sense of every action. Or, rather, not even the sense, but the meaning."

"Evidently you've devoted much time to reflecting on this question. You've probably had occasion to think to what degree your own life…"

He suddenly grew much paler. The violins played a piercing shriek.

"Many years ago," he said, "I met my death; I saw it as clearly as the Persian gardener. However, by an unusual twist of fate, it passed by me. *Elle m'a raté.* I don't know how to say it any differently. I was very young; I was racing towards it at breakneck speed, but this twist of fate I mention saved me. Now I'm travelling towards it slowly; I essentially ought to be grateful that it seems to have skipped a page, since it's given me the good fortune of gazing into your eyes and expounding upon these semi-philosophical snatches."

"It seemed to me then that everything was against me," said Yelena Nikolayevna. "The night, the music, that face with those sparkling eyes. But still I had enough strength to resist this. It didn't hold out for long, though."

She would meet him around once a week. After their initial meeting in the restaurant, there was a period when he shed what she termed his philosophical manner—he spoke of horse racing, films, books, and the more she learnt of him, the more apparent it became to her that he was by far superior to all those whom she had encountered before. Nevertheless, despite all these clever, true things, despite the fact that a whole world, previously unknown to her, was opening before her very eyes, a film of cold, quiet despair shrouded everything. She never stopped resisting this internally. She couldn't counter his reasoning with anything else; it would have been too unequal an argument, and the outcome would have been inevitable. However, all her being protested against this; she knew that it was not right, or, if it were right, it was necessary to make some superhuman effort to forget it immediately and never return to him.

"Every love affair is an attempt to thwart fate; it's a naive illusion of brief immortality," he once said. "Nevertheless, it's probably the best thing that we're ever given to know. But it's easy to see the slow work of death even in this. '*Vouloir nous brûle et pouvoir nous détruit.*' You'll find that in Balzac's *La Peau de chagrin.*"

She asked herself the question: what has given this

man the strength to live? That in which others believed didn't exist for him; even the best, most wonderful things lost their charm as soon as he touched them. And yet his attractiveness was irresistible. Yelena Nikolayevna knew that it was inevitable, and, when she became his lover, it seemed to her as though she were recalling something that had already taken place long ago. Sometime later she came to understand just how this man was able to exist and what had supported him on his long journey towards death: he was a morphine addict. She once asked him how it could be that he, with his intellect and abilities, a man head and shoulders above all the others she had known, could have reached such a hopeless situation.

"It's because I missed my own death," he replied.

Her affair with him was clouded by yet another tragic event. His former lover, the mistress of the house in which Yelena Nikolayevna had first heard Scriabin's music, could not come to terms with her new-found status. She wrote menacing letters, threatened to expose them, lay in wait by the entrance to his building for hours on end. She was an absurd woman, who, as he put it, had lived her life forever in thought of some nonsense or other; then she fell in love with him, and in doing so fulfilled her own existence. Had he ever loved her? No, it had been a lengthy misunderstanding. However, it ended in tragedy: she poisoned herself, leaving her husband a detailed letter, in which she divulged the story of her affair and explained that she was depriving herself of life because this man no longer wanted to be with her. With naive cruelty, she added: "You—the man who loved me so dearly—you of all people must understand what this meant."

He tried to hook Yelena Nikolayevna on morphine—this was essentially the only thing in which he did not succeed. After her first attempt, she claimed to feel an icy and until then incomprehensible transparency; later on she felt faint, however, and never repeated the endeavour. In all other aspects she felt as if she were growing weaker and would ultimately perish. She gradually began to take for granted all the things she had first thought of as interesting, like the possibility of a new understanding of the world. What she had considered important and fundamental throughout her whole life now seemed uncontrollably to be losing its value once and for all. She was ceasing to love the things she had once loved. It seemed as though everything was withering and now all that occasionally remained was some sort of deathly adulation followed by a void. Whole years of wearisome life seemed to separate her from their first meeting, and she felt as if nothing in her remained of the former Lenochka, the woman she had been not so long ago. Even her character changed; her movements became more sluggish, her reactions to what was going on around her lost their sharpness; in short, it was as if she were suffering from some deep psychological affliction. She felt that it would all end in oblivion or else a plunge into some frozen abyss if it were to go on any longer. Her attempts to change his life— for she undoubtedly did love him—led to nothing. And the warmth inside her gradually grew weaker and disappeared.

And just as a man, half poisoned by gas and about to

lose consciousness, finds the strength to crawl to the window and open it, so, too, waking up one morning, did she find the strength to pack her things and go to the railway station, and thence onwards to Paris. Before this, however, she did everything she could to try to return him to a normal life. She told me of her last conversation with him. It took place one evening, at his apartment. He was sitting in an armchair; his face was tired and his eyes lacklustre. She said to him:

"Everything in your life is somehow so hideous that I can't go on any more. You say you love me?"

He nodded.

"Have you considered that I might have a child?"

"No."

"I believe I have the right to be a mother just as much as any other woman."

He shrugged his shoulders.

"I could have married you. Even then, it's clearly absurd. Neither one is impossible. Why? You think you're condemned to death. But we're all condemned to death."

"Not quite."

"Why not?"

"Because everyone comprehends this only theoretically, whereas I know it for a fact. How? I cannot explain. In some prisons, the prisoners are released into the town for a day or two on their word of honour. They dress like everyone else, they are free to dine in a restaurant or visit a theatre. But they're still different, aren't they? I've been let out for a certain time, but I can neither think nor live as everyone else does, because I know what awaits me."

"This is a form of madness."

"Perhaps. But what is madness, anyway?"

"In any case, you understand that this cannot continue. I cannot live like this."

"You'd think any other life uninteresting and dreary now. You'll never regain what you once were."

"Why?"

"Firstly, because that's hardly likely."

"And secondly?"

"Secondly, because I won't allow it."

"You mean to say you'll stop me?"

"Yes."

"How?"

"That's unimportant. However I wish."

Had it not been for this conversation, she would most likely have stayed on with him for a certain period. However, she could not bear the thought that she might be forced into something or held back by some sort of threat.

Having left him, she became convinced that there had been a significant amount of truth in his words. She had been poisoned by his intimacy, perhaps for a long time, perhaps for ever. It was as if only now, for the first time in all these months and years, she felt that perhaps not all was lost. She literally spoke the words:

"And only now am I beginning to think that perhaps not all is lost."

I stepped away from the window and sat down next to her on the divan.

"How warm you are," she said.

"Of course, he doesn't know where you are, does he?"

"No, he only knows that I left. I don't think he'd be able to find me. May I lie down? Telling you all this has worn me out. Yet I always knew that one day I'd tell someone about my life, because he'd ask me about it and because in those few moments I'd love him. Do you see how long I've known about you?"

"Yes, of course. Just as one day you'll tell someone about me. And you'll say: 'He wrote obituaries, and reports on sports matches, and articles about a women cut up into pieces'—and what else, Lenochka?"

"What else? That you understood more than you knew how to say, and that the tone of your voice was more expressive than the words you spoke. Though perhaps I shan't say this to anyone."

Once more I found myself walking home through the empty night-time streets, and, despite my wanting to fall asleep and forget everything, I couldn't help reflecting on this man whom Yelena Nikolayevna had mentioned. What could have befallen him that brought about this terrible psychological affliction? I knew that searching for the moment of any mental ailment's inception was always a tortuous process and, more often than not, totally futile. Yet, even if I were to find the correct answer to this question beyond all doubt, I would have no means of verifying it. Then again, what did I have to do with this man in the first place? It only confirmed to me afresh that by recurring chance, or perhaps on account of some other reasons of which I was unaware, every one of my affairs always contained some unnecessarily tragic element, and this was almost without exception through no fault of my own. I would often find myself grudgingly paying the price for one of my predecessors. In some instances, Fate was especially derisive in its dealings with me. I could never forget one woman I was seeing, remarkable in many respects, but outstanding for her unspeakably hellish nature. I spent several years with her; feeling truly sorry for her, I did everything so that she might be less unfortunate, since she herself was the primary victim of her own flaws. A prolonged period of mental calm ultimately had a favourable effect on her—and after this she left me, insisting all the while that she harboured no ill feeling towards me and, with unconscious artlessness, believing that this alone should seem like an almost unmerited happiness to me. After a certain period, her new lover, by all accounts a rather nice chap, informed me that she had told him a great deal about me, that he was very pleased to make my acquaintance, and that she was a remarkable woman with a perfect disposition—a thing so very rare, as he remarked, in our neurotic age.

It began to seem as though my role was limited to appearing on the scene after a catastrophe, and that everyone to whom I was destined to have any emotional attachment would have undoubtedly fallen victim to some sort of prior misfortune. In certain cases this took on a more tragic note, in others, less so. It was always difficult, however, and matters would be further complicated by the fact that each time, through an old, unhealthy habit of which I could not rid myself, I would mull everything over and over at great length, rejecting things as they were, and constructing around them a whole system of my own vain notions about how they could be, had circumstances only been otherwise. I always sought to find the reasons for a catastrophe—and so now I thought of my predecessor in London, of this man who had such an inscrutable bent for anything that involved the notion of death. What could account for the development of such a psychological affliction? I had absolutely no facts upon which to base any judgement. But the question interested me mainly from a purely theoretical perspective, as any arbitrary psychological problem might do. Judging by his age—Yelena Nikolayevna once said that he was around ten years older than I—he would have probably fought in the war, so perhaps this had affected him in some way. I knew both from personal experience and by the example of many of my comrades that fighting in a war has an irreparably destructive effect on almost any man. I knew also that the constant proximity of death, the sight of the killed, wounded, dying, hanged and shot, the great red flame in the icy air above blazing villages on a winter's night, the carcass of a man's horse and those auditory impressions—the alarm bell, shell explosions, the whistle of bullets, the desperate, unknown cries—none of this ever passes with impunity. I knew that the silent, almost unconscious memory of war haunts the majority of people who have gone through it, leaving something broken in them once and for all. I knew myself that the normal, human ideas regarding the value of life and the necessity for a basic moral code—not to kill, not to steal, not to rape, to show compassion—had been slowly reasserted within me after the war, but they had lost their former persuasiveness and had become merely a system of theoretical morality, with whose correctness and necessity I couldn't, in principle, disagree. Those feelings that ought to have been inside me and that were a condition of the re-establishment of this code had been razed by war; they no longer existed, and there was nothing to take their place.

He must, of course, have known everything that I knew about this. On the other hand, hundreds of thousands of people had gone through war without going mad. No, of course, it was more natural to suppose that some particular events had occurred in his life, of which even Yelena Nikolayevna was unaware and which predetermined his current situation. What, for example, did he mean by "*elle m'a raté*"? In any case, Yelena Nikolayevna's eyes were frozen over with a fixed, unnaturally calm expression, like a forgotten reflection in a mirror—and it bore a direct relation to me, although not in the same way as everything else did, because unfortunately everything else, too, related to me. At the time, and particularly that night, returning home, I felt an unusual irritation at the impossibility of escaping the world of objects, thoughts and memories, the chaotic and silent movement of which accompanied my whole life. Sometimes I felt ready to curse my memory, which retained so many things whose absence would have made my life much easier. It was impossible to change this, however, and only in my life's rarest moments, ones that demanded of me the greatest mental effort, would all this leave me for a time, merely to return again later.

I made half the journey on foot, then hailed a passing taxi; soon after arriving home, I was fast asleep.

I recall that the weather was splendid the following day: sun and blue skies with white feathery clouds. I was in fine spirits for working, and within a few hours I had managed to write a substantial article, this time not about crime or bankruptcy, but about a few characteristics of Maupassant's. That evening, when I was at Yelena Nikolayevna's, she told me that she felt several years younger; she, too, was evidently yielding to that same involuntary motion again, as had happened in the beginning, on the day of my first visit to her and during the week preceding it.

One day, having worked together into the early afternoon, she informed me that she had been invited to the theatre that evening and that we would see each other only the following morning. "I'll wake you at daybreak," she said, leaving. I knew that she was going to the theatre with an old friend of hers, whom she had met by chance in Paris. I had seen her two or three times: she was a portly woman, but rather pretty. For some reason, laying eyes on her would never fail to whet my appetite, no matter when it happened. Even after a substantial breakfast, the sight of her would always call to mind the thought of food; if I were to close my eyes, vague apparitions of hams, sturgeon, salmon and lobsters would emerge out of the darkness. This woman unknowingly brought with her a whole world of gastronomic visions, of which she was the sole cause. I could never reach any definitive conclusion when trying to analyse precisely why this happened, and as we had no mutual acquaintances I could not even ascertain whether other people shared this impression or whether it was the result of my personal (and thus all the more incomprehensible) distortion. She had married a Frenchman: a very charming man, though lacking in personality.

"Come here, if you like. Annie will feed you," said Yelena Nikolayevna.

I declined, and at half past nine in the evening I set out for the Russian restaurant. As I approached, I thought of Voznesensky and the Gypsy love songs. I walked in and spotted him at once. He was not alone: at his table, with his back to me, sat a man in a light-grey suit; his fair hair did not quite manage to cover his incipient bald patch. Voznesensky waved to me and stood up from his chair, inviting me over. When I reached the table, he said:

"I'm truly glad to see you, my dear chap. Here, permit me to introduce you: Sasha Wolf, in the flesh, or, if you will, Alexander Andreyevich, just in from London. Another decanter please, my beauty," he said, turning to the waitress who had arrived at the table at the same time as I, "and do be liberal, my dear."

Alexander Wolf turned his head, allowing me to see his face. He was still handsome; to look at, one might have guessed he was around forty. Perhaps, had I not known that it was him, I might not have paid him any particular attention. However, I knew beyond all doubt that here, right in front of me, I was looking at that long-familiar face, whose memory had haunted me for so many years. He had very fair skin and still, grey eyes.

"I've been telling him about you," said Voznesensky. "Were it not for him, Sasha, I'd never have found out what it was you wrote in that book of yours. Sit down, dear fellow, let's have a glass; we are Orthodox, after all."

I couldn't find the words to strike up a conversation with Wolf. I had imagined this meeting for such a long time; I wanted to say so many things that I scarcely knew where to begin. Besides, Voznesensky's presence, the restaurant's surroundings and all those glasses of vodka did not befit the conversation I had envisaged. Alexander Wolf spoke little and limited himself to making brief remarks. Voznesensky, on the other hand, would not stop. As soon as I sat down at the table, he drank another glass and began staring drunkenly at Wolf.

"Sasha, my friend," he said with uncommon expressiveness in his voice, "just think who you are to me. I have no better friend. We were really about to cart you off dead, you son of a bitch, but the doctor patched you up in hospital. Now, is that true or not? And if it is, then who did Marina leave me for, eh? What a girl she was, Sasha! Did you ever know a better one?"

"I did," said Wolf with unexpected certainty.

"You're lying. That cannot be, Sasha. I haven't and never will. Why don't you write about her, even if it is in English? She's good in every language. Write, Sasha, be a good chap."

Wolf looked plainly at him, then shifted his gaze onto me.

"I was interested in your story 'The Adventure in the Steppe'," I said, "for several reasons, which I'll relate to you, if I might, in more suitable surroundings. In any case, I'd like to speak to you on a number of matters that are important, at least, from my perspective."

"At your service," he replied. "If you'd like, we can meet here the day after tomorrow, at around five o'clock. Vladimir Petrovich has told me all about his conversations with you."

"Very well," I said. "Here, the day after tomorrow, at five o'clock."

I didn't leave at once. Whenever I had the chance, I would look at Wolf with that typical avid, fixed intensity, which had only recently diminished as other, stronger feelings had taken hold of me. I made efforts to visualize him as he might have appeared, had I known nothing at all about him; I tried to detach myself from those fixed ideas that had for too long haunted my imagination and were interfering with me at that very moment. However, I could not say with certainty to what degree I was successful in my attempt. There was something in Wolf's face, I thought, that distinguished it from the other faces I saw. It was an obscure expression, some sort of deathly significance—a look that seemed entirely impossible on the face of any living man. To anyone who had read his book as closely as I had, it seemed especially peculiar that this man, with his fixed gaze and indescribable expression, could have written such quick-paced, taut prose and seen so many things through those motionless eyes.

"Beneath me lay my corpse, with the arrow in my

temple"—I suddenly remembered the epigraph to "The Adventure in the Steppe". That was just it: he really did look like a spectre. How could I have failed to realize this right from the very start? Suddenly, a cold chill passed through me. And again the voice of the gramophone sang out Voznesensky's favourite romance:

> There's no need for anything,
> Not even late regrets…

I remembered envisaging this very scene long ago: the restaurant, the music and (through the drunken Gypsy sorrow) the lifeless face belonging to the unknown author of *I'll Come Tomorrow*. I closed my eyes; before me swirled an incredible assemblage of thoughts, memories and emotions, and everything filtered through those motifs and imaginary melodies I had thought of when I pictured Marina singing to Sasha Wolf's accompaniment. Then, as if in a dream, I saw the black foresight of a revolver swaying in front of my right eye with extraordinary clarity. I felt a chill; delirium appeared to be setting in.

I finally got up and left, in spite of Voznesensky's loud protestations. He reached out towards me, holding up a glass of vodka, trying to persuade me to sit back down awhile before heading somewhere else. I hinted at some pressing work; otherwise I might have found difficulty in refusing his persistent invitations. Anything pertaining to literature or journalism assumed an almost sacred meaning for him, and no state of intoxication could alter this.

"In that case, dear fellow, I wouldn't dare detain you any further," he said. "Best of luck with your endeavours."

I left the restaurant, but felt disinclined to go home straight away. I walked along rue de la Convention, heading towards the Seine. It was around half past eleven in the evening and still quite warm; there was a rattle from the trees, which had recently come into leaf and not yet managed to acquire that languid, dusty look they take on in summer. I was left with a feeling of unease after my encounter with Wolf, and for the hundredth time I called to mind everything that was connected with him—from the moment he had fallen to the road, to the book he had written and my meeting with the publisher in London who hated him so vehemently. I thought about how Wolf had become—and not so much Wolf personally as the very thought of him—the involuntary personification of everything dead and sad that existed in my life. This was supplemented by an awareness of my own guilt: I felt like a murderer standing beside the body of his victim, shocked by the crime he has just committed. And although I was no murderer and Wolf was no corpse, I couldn't distance myself from this notion. What am I really guilty of? I asked myself. Despite supposing that any court would acquit me—a military court, because killing is the law and purpose of war; a civil court, because I'd acted in self-defence—something eternally onerous remained in all this. I never meant to kill him; I saw him for the first time only a moment before I fired. Why, then, did the very thought of him comprise such unshakable regret, such insurmountable sorrow?

The reason I had grown aware of this non-existent guilt

now became clear to me: it was that thought of murder that had occupied my imagination so many times with such a commanding greed. It hit me with the same unexpectedness that had caused me only half an hour ago in the restaurant to realize what made Wolf so unlike others: his unexpected appearance coinciding with the idea of his spectrality. Perhaps it was like the final glimmer of a dying flame, a fleeting return to ancient instinct; perhaps again it was some curious manifestation of the laws of heredity. I knew that murder and revenge had been a constant, obligatory tradition for countless generations of my forebears. This combination of allure and aversion, this unshakable bent towards criminality, had seemingly always resided within me; realizing this, of course, was the reason for the bitter regret I now felt. The thought of Wolf was the strongest reminder of this trait, a theoretically criminal detail in my psychological portrait. Had Wolf never existed, it would have remained in the realms of my imagination, and I could have sustained the comforting illusion that all this was simply the result of fantasy and that, if it were to happen in reality, I would find sufficient inner strength to refrain from that final, irreversible act. Wolf's existence deprived me of this vain illusion. Anyway, if this one shot had cost me so much, its consequences must have affected Wolf's entire life, too. Once again, comparing my vision of the author of *I'll Come Tomorrow* with everything that Voznesensky had told me, I thought that perhaps, were it not for this unfinished murder, a happy life might have awaited Sasha Wolf, and those dismal things described in Alexander Wolf's book would have remained unknown. I mulled things over—how many times had I done so?—and recalled the words uttered by Yelena Nikolayevna's lover in London:

"The chain of events in each human life is miraculous."

Yes, of course, and if I were to introduce the Law of Causality as an explanatory element into this complex aggregate of varied and simultaneous occurrences, the wonder of what happened would appear even more evident, and it would seem as though a whole world had sprung into existence from a single action of mine. Assuming that the origin of this long chain of events was my outstretched hand holding a revolver and the bullet that pierced Wolf's chest, then in this brief space of time, as quick as a flash, a complex process was born, which could be neither foreseen nor accounted for by any human mind possessed of even the most powerful, grotesque imagination. Who could have known that the bullet's spinning, instantaneous flight actually contained that town on the Dnieper, Marina's inexpressible charm, her bracelets, her singing, her betrayal, her disappearance, Voznesensky's life, the ship's hold, Constantinople, London, Paris, the book *I'll Come Tomorrow* and the epigraph about the corpse with the arrow in its temple?

Leaving Yelena Nikolayevna's apartment the following night, I said to her:

"I don't know when I'll come tomorrow, or even whether I'll come at all. I'll telephone."

"Has something happened?"

"No, but I have an important engagement."

"With a man or a woman?"

"With a spectre," I said. "I'll tell you about it later."

When I entered, there was no one in the restaurant other than a drunken taxi driver, who was ceaselessly kissing the waitress's proffered hand and telling her about his exploits. I arrived at ten to five. Wolf was not there yet, and so I managed to catch exactly what the driver was saying. He was a gallant man—gallant really was the word—a former cavalryman, exceedingly amiable (at least in his drunken state) and, in his own countrified way, disarmingly high society.

As I sat drinking coffee, I head him say:

"So then I wrote her a letter. I wrote: 'What's to be done, my dearest? Our paths have gone in different directions.' But I added a phrase that she's never likely to forget."

"Which was that?" asked the waitress.

"I wrote precisely this: 'I placed you on such a high pedestal; you came down from it yourself.'"

Just then, Wolf entered the restaurant. He was wearing a different suit, one of navy blue. I shook his hand. He ordered some coffee for himself and looked at me calmly and expectantly. Despite having debated at length how best to begin the conversation and what to say afterwards, nothing came out as I'd imagined it would. But that, of course, was of no import.

"A few months ago," I said, "at this very table, Vladimir Petrovich told me of his acquaintance with you. This came after my first attempt to find something out about you—I'll mention that later, if I may—met with a most unexpected failure."

"What exactly brought about, on your part, such an interest in my person?" he enquired. Again, I couldn't help noticing his voice, very flat and inexpressive, without any sharp changes of intonation.

I extracted his book from my briefcase, opened it at the page where "The Adventure in the Steppe" began, and said:

"As you'll recall, your story begins with a reference to a white stallion of Apocalyptic beauty, which the protagonist is riding towards death. After the events described next, the protagonist asks himself what might have happened to the man who shot him, the man who continued galloping towards death on that same horse, while he, the protagonist, lay dying across the road with a bullet just above his heart. Isn't that so?"

Wolf gazed at me intently, slightly narrowing his unmoving eyes.

"Yes. What of it?"

"I can answer that question for you," I said.

His face didn't change; only his eyes became narrower still.

"You can answer that question?"

My breathing became laboured, and I felt a strange tightening in my chest.

"I remember it as if it were yesterday," I said. "It was I who shot you."

Wolf suddenly got up from his chair and remained

standing for a second, as if intending to do something significant. Straight away, he seemed to have grown taller by a whole head. And then I caught sight of his eyes, so wide and still; something truly terrible flashed in them. It hit me instantly that lurking within the author of *I'll Come Tomorrow* there was still a trace of something almost forgotten, almost dead, but precisely what Voznesensky had once known so well, something that I had halted back then only because I had a revolver, and only because I had been capable of becoming a murderer. But Wolf sat down straight away, saying:

"Please, do excuse me. I'm listening."

"It was my face that you saw after you fell from your horse. You weren't mistaken in your description of me: I was sixteen years old at the time. I must have looked so tired; I hadn't slept for thirty hours. It was I who rode off on your white stallion—you'd killed my black mare with your first shot. I was the one who stood there, leaning over you. And I was in a rush to leave because I'd caught the distant sound of hooves on the wind. More recently, I learnt from Vladimir Petrovich that the sound had come from the horses that he and two of his comrades were riding, in search of you."

Wolf remained silent. The driver, completely drunk, was telling the story of his letter again, but now to a different waitress.

"…such a high pedestal; you came down from it yourself…"

"So, it's you," said Wolf in an assertive tone of voice.

"I'm afraid so," I replied. "All these years the memory has never left me. I paid very dearly for that shot. Even my happiest moments were clouded by some sort of dark, empty space where I could always find that same mortal regret for having killed you. I'm sure you'll understand how happy it made me to read your story and realize that in fact you hadn't died. So, I hope you'll forgive me now for my rashness in seeking out the author of *I'll Come Tomorrow*."

I was waiting for him to respond. He said nothing. When he took a deep breath, I noticed that he was evidently as excited as I was. He said:

"It's so unexpected; I'd imagined you so differently, and I'd grown so used to the thought that you were long dead…"

Voznesensky appeared in the doorway. Wolf said to me quickly:

"We'll talk about this tomorrow, here, at the same time. All right?"

I nodded.

Voznesensky was in particularly high spirits that day. He slapped Wolf on the back, shook my hand and sat down. When the waitress set down a decanter of vodka and began to lay the table, he poured three glasses, saying:

"Well, Sasha, here's to you. And you, dear friend: who knows what the future holds for us?"

Wolf was preoccupied and said nothing.

"England, or no England," said Voznesensky after his fourth glass, "they say the people there really know how to drink. I'll readily accept that. But here I am, a simple Russian man, and you won't frighten me with any England. Sit me down to drink with any Englishman, and then we'll see."

He then shot me a look of reproach.

"Whereas our friend here is more of the snacking sort. Of course, one needn't starve to death in a restaurant—God forbid!—but drinking is what counts."

When the gramophone began to play, Voznesensky, who knew all the romances, sang along in his deep voice. After the fifth record, Wolf said:

"You're tireless, Volodya; you ought to take a break."

"My good man," said Voznesensky, shrugging his shoulders, "what is there to take a break from? I, Sasha, haven't forgotten my roots; so many of my ancestors sang till their throats were hoarse that all this is a mere trifle for me."

After we finished eating, I realized that my head was spinning, even though I hadn't drunk that much. Voznesensky suggested taking a stroll (as he put it), but no sooner had we stepped out onto the street than he hailed the first taxi that came along, and we set off for Montmartre. There we began making our way round all the various spots, and little by little everything became jumbled in my mind. I remembered afterwards how there had been some nude mulatto women—their guttural chatter faintly reaching my ears—and other girls in varying states of undress. Swarthy youths of a southern sort had been playing guitars, and at one point there was Negro singing and a deafening jazz band. An enormous Negress had performed a belly dance with unusual artistry; as I watched her, she seemed to be made up of separate pieces of elastic black flesh moving independently of one another, as though the spectacle were taking place in some monstrous dissecting room that had suddenly sprung to life. Then came more music: the strumming of ukuleles. Holding a tumbler containing a whitish-green liquid, Voznesensky said:

"He who has been to Tahiti will surely return there to die."

His rich baritone voice joined in the singing, and he added:

"What is a northern woman? The sun's reflection on ice."

His inebriation was of a benign and erotic nature; he drank to the health of all his short-run companionesses and was, it seemed, completely happy.

Later, all these exotic scenes were replaced by more European entertainments—Hungarian Gypsies sang, French artistes performed. When we left a cabaret somewhere near boulevard Rochechouart, there was a street fight going on between some shady individuals; women were taking part and shouting in their fierce, shrill voices. I stood next to Wolf; the street lamp cast a harsh light on his pale face, which seemed to bear an expression of quiet despair. I felt as if I were gazing at this wild, strange crowd with distant eyes, as though from some far-off vantage point; I even imagined that I was hearing incoherent cries in an unknown tongue, although, naturally, I was familiar with all the words and nuances of the argot used by these pimps and prostitutes. I felt an agonizing disgust, which combined mysteriously with an intensified interest in this scuffle. It was, however, brought swiftly to an end by a whole array of policemen, who placed a score of bloodied men and women into three huge trucks and quickly drove off. On the pavement there remained a few half-trampled caps and—quite how it was lost by one of the participants in the fight is unclear—a pink brassiere. And while these details did seem to impart a certain convincingness to everything I had witnessed that night, I was still unable to rid myself of the impression that this evening stroll had been a patent fantasy, as though in the habitual quiet of my imagination I had been walking around a strange, unfamiliar city, alongside the spectre haunting this long, uninterrupted dream.

The sun was beginning to rise; we were walking home. We sauntered through the dim mix of lamplight and dawn, down the steep streets descending from Montmartre. After such a noisy and tiring evening, I found it difficult to follow what Wolf was saying. I do, however, remember some snatches of conversation. He was interesting to talk to, he knew a great deal and saw everything in a very distinct light, and so gradually I came to understand how this man could have written such a book. That night, I gained the impression that he was fundamentally indifferent to all earthly matters: he spoke as though nothing could possibly have any direct bearing on him. His philosophy was distinguished for its dearth of illusion: individual destiny was unimportant, for we each always carry our own death—that is to say, the generally instantaneous termination of life's habitual rhythm. Every day, dozens of worlds are born and dozens of others die, and yet we pass through these invisible cosmic catastrophes, mistakenly supposing the modest little area

that falls within our field of vision to be some sort of rep-
lica of the whole world in miniature. Still, he believed in
some elusive system of general laws, far removed, however,
from an idyllic state of harmony: what seems like blind
chance to us is most often inevitability. He theorized that
logic couldn't exist outside conditional, arbitrary, almost
mathematical constructs, and that death and happiness
were fundamentally of the same order, as both one and
the other involve the same notion of fixity.

"And what of the thousands of happy lives out there?"

"Yes, people living like blind puppies."

"Not necessarily."

"If we're possessed of that tragic, ferocious courage that
forces man to live with his eyes open, can we really ever be
happy? It's impossible even to imagine that the world's most
extraordinary people were happy. Shakespeare couldn't
have been happy. Nor could Michelangelo."

"What about St Francis of Assisi?"

We were crossing a bridge over the Seine. An early-
morning mist hung above the river; through it, one could
just about glimpse the semi-spectral city.

"He loved the world as people love little children," said
Wolf. "But I'm not sure that he was happy. Remember
that Christ was everlastingly sad; Christianity is altogether
inconceivable without this sadness."

Then he added in a different tone of voice:

"It's always seemed to me that life is somehow like a train
journey: the slowness of individual existence, imprisoned
within an impetuous outer motion; that apparent safety,

that semblance of duration. And then, in a split second, a collapsed bridge or a loose rail, and that same termination of rhythm—death."

"Is that how you imagine it?"

"Do you see it any differently?"

"I don't know. But if it weren't for this violent termination of rhythm, as you call it, then perhaps it could be different: a slow departure, a gradual cooling and an almost imperceptible, painless slide into a world where the word 'rhythm' is probably meaningless."

"To each man, of course, his own death; however, his conception of it can be mistaken. I, for example, am sure that I'll die just like that—suddenly and violently, in much the same way as when we first met. I'm convinced of it, despite its improbability amid the peaceful, happy circumstances of my present life."

We parted at length, and then I went home. As there had still been no discussion of the main issue—that being "The Adventure in the Steppe"—we agreed to meet in the restaurant at three o'clock the following afternoon.

During the meeting Wolf seemed a little livelier than before; there was a spring in his step, and this time I didn't notice the usual, distant expression in his eyes. Only his voice remained as flat and inexpressive as always.

I told him of my fruitless attempts to find out the information that had interested me, making special reference to the visit I paid the director of the publishing house in London. I felt bound to tell Wolf how I had been astonished by this man's parting words to me.

"I must admit," replied Wolf, "that he does have some grounds to speak in that vein. He held me responsible for a certain, very tragic, episode. Unfortunately, I cannot go into any detail on the matter; I have no right to do so. His opinion of me was, on the whole, mistaken, but I quite understand it."

"There's still one aspect of this that I cannot fathom," I said. "It's something that's difficult to account for purely in psychological terms, if you will. I never doubted that Vladimir Petrovich's version of Sasha Wolf corresponded with reality, but how could that same Sasha Wolf, partisan and adventurer, write the book *I'll Come Tomorrow*?"

He smiled grimly, using only his lips.

"Sasha Wolf, of course, couldn't have written *I'll Come Tomorrow*; I don't believe he could have written anything at all. However, he ceased to exist a long time ago: it was a different man who wrote this book. I think you have to believe in fate. Thus you'll also believe, with that same classic naivety, that you've been its pawn. Then everything falls into place: chance, the shot, your sixteen years of age, your youthful aim, and this same"—he touched me below the shoulder—"unshaking hand."

I unwittingly thought how wild his words sounded. We were sitting in the Russian restaurant; I could hear the clatter of crockery and the chef's angry voice coming from the kitchen:

"I told her—schnitzel first, push the schnitzel."

"You said you remembered everything as if it were yesterday. I, too, remember everything. I thought you were frozen with fear after you got up from the fall and just stood there. Weren't you afraid?"

"Apparently not. At first I was stunned, but I don't have a clear memory of what happened next; I was so desperate for sleep, and all my strength was being sapped in the struggle with that desire. At any rate, I'm not afraid of death, or, rather, life has never seemed all that precious to me."

"And yet it's the sole thing whose value we can truly comprehend."

I looked at him in astonishment. Such a phrase sounded particularly unexpected coming from his lips.

"I realized this as I lay dying on the road. In those few moments it seemed clear to me—clear to the point of blinding me. But later I could never recapture this feeling, and because I could never recapture it, I turned into the author of that book. I waited my whole life for something unexpected to happen, something entirely unforeseen, some incredible shock, when I'd see anew what I'd once loved so much: the warm, sensual world that I lost. I don't know why it slipped away from me. But it happened at that very moment. I cannot tell you how terrible it was, the disappearance of the world I was living in: the road, the sun, and your sleepy eyes looking down on me. I thought you'd have died long ago. I pitied you; you were my companion, and yet you fell into some abyss of time and distance, and I was the only person to have seen your departure. Had I been able

134

to speak, I'd have shouted to you to stop, that it was waiting for you, as it had been waiting for me, and that it wouldn't miss a second time. And so, you see, I'd have been wrong. If you only knew how many times I thought about you! I wanted to turn back time. I wished I hadn't your death on my conscience, that I hadn't made a murderer of you."

"I, too, often thought about this," I said. "I'd have given so much not to have been haunted all these years by your spectre."

"How hypothetical all this is!" said Wolf. "You were convinced that you'd killed me, I was sure that you'd died as a result of my actions, and yet neither of us was right. But what difference does it make, I ask, right or wrong, when you spent so many years in vain regret, and I waiting for a second miracle? Who will give us back the time, and who will change your fate or mine? And do you think, after all this, that it's still possible to harbour any naive illusions?"

"It is possible to understand that all illusions are vain and that in the end there's no consolation. Firstly, however, that doesn't help matters, and, secondly, if we were incapable of even the smallest, most insignificant illusion, then all we'd be left with is what you call the termination of a rhythm. So, as we're still alive, perhaps not all is lost."

Wolf remained silent awhile; he sat with his head lowered, propped up by both his hands, like a schoolboy trying to solve a difficult problem. When he raised his eyes to me, I once again glimpsed that same terrible expression I first saw after revealing that it was I who had shot him. Oddly, however, his manner towards me didn't tally with this.

"My dear friend," he said, "do you know why I came to Paris?"

What further admission could this man possibly make?

"The solution to a complex psychological problem rests on my stay here. It has a twofold interest: a personal one, which is of the utmost importance, and an abstract one, which isn't entirely devoid of meaning either."

"Forgive me for asking, but to what extent does the solution depend on you personally?"

"In its entirety."

"Then it isn't a problem."

"*Un cas de conscience*, if you will. But there's no greater temptation than that of forcing events to take the course you wish, stopping at nothing to achieve this."

"And if that should prove impossible?…"

"Then all that remains is to destroy the cause of these events. It's one solution, certainly, albeit the least desirable."

I left the restaurant immediately after Wolf. I saw him hail a taxi and get into the vehicle. Then, with a sobbing sound, I heard the door gently slam shut. It was a warm day in May, and the sun was shining brilliantly; it was around five o'clock in the afternoon.

I returned home and sat down at my writing desk, but I was unable to work. I closed my eyes, and before me appeared the distorted face of the publisher in London. "Of course, one must take into consideration the exceptional circumstances and your age at the time. But if your shot had been more accurate…"—"Beneath me lay my corpse, with the arrow in my temple…" Once again I saw the forest and the road—it was right there, in my room, reaching me across the vastness that separated me from far-off southern Russia. I felt truly sorry for Wolf. "The world that I lost I know not why." And then this comforting philosophy: every day we pass through cosmic catastrophes, but the misfortune lies in that the cosmic catastrophes leave us indifferent, whereas the slightest change in our own insignificant life can provoke our pain or regret, and yet there's nothing to be done about this. "Who will give us back the time?" No one, of course. However, if it were possible to work this miracle, we would surely find ourselves in someone else's strange, distant life, and who knows whether it would be better than our own. And what does "better" mean, anyway? The life to which we're destined can be no otherwise; no power is able to alter it, even happiness, which is of the same order as death, as it contains that element of fixity. Without fixity there can be no happiness—the very thing that some Oriental ruler was unable to find "in the books of wisdom, on the back of a horse, or even at the breast of a woman." Lenochka might say: "Later, when you and I are no longer together and I have another lover..." Perhaps she won't tell him anything about me, perhaps she'll remark laconically: "I was having an affair with a certain man at the time," and this single phrase will encompass all those nights when she belonged to me, her flushed face, her breasts squeezed in my embrace, her grimace at the final moment, and everything that came before it. All this will be followed by someone else's embraces and again that voice of hers with those same, almost impersonal intonations, the voice

137

she used when speaking to me and, before this, to others; it had probably always sounded just as sincere. What a wealth of sensual possibility, and what poverty of expression! Yes, of course, even the most wonderful girl cannot give more than she has. Most of the time, though, she has enough spirit to allow us to construct and imagine her; it was on account of this that Dulcinea was beyond comparison. It's another delusion to think that reality is more just than imagination. Perhaps, though, Lenochka doesn't merit my censure: what's to prevent me from thinking that she'll for ever belong solely to me, that she's loved no one other than me, and that if she believes she did or will, it's a monstrous and patent error, even if she doesn't understand it herself? And if parting and betrayal were inevitable, there was still a period of time in which the whole fabric of her being would belong to me, and that was the main thing. Thereafter, there would be only fragments: these would fall to the lot of others, and these others would never know what she had given to me—all the spiritual and physical riches that I accepted from her as a gift. What more could remain of her after this? Suddenly, I felt her presence so close to me that I developed the absurd desire to turn my head to see whether or not she was really there; so distinctly could I sense her perfume, the movement of her body under a dress; I thought I could see her eyes and hear those abrupt falling intonations in her voice, which my indebted memory had preserved for ever. I loved her more than anyone else and naturally more than myself, and so, for once in my life, on account of this desire for her, I was drawing nearer to the

Gospel ideal—that is, if the Gospel had ever spoken of such love. "Remember that Christ was everlastingly sad." And there again was the spectre of Alexander Wolf. There was something about the author of *I'll Come Tomorrow* that I didn't want to dwell on; however, I had to see this through to the end. I felt a constant sense of guilt for what I'd done to him. Yes, undoubtedly so. Twice I'd marked that terrible expression in his eyes: for the first time when he learnt that it was I who shot him, and later when he said to me, "My dear friend..." Of course, back then in Russia it was he who'd ultimately come galloping after me on his white stallion: in fact I ought to have been the victim, not he. But then, it wasn't without reason that he kept returning the conversation to this instantaneous and violent termination of rhythm—most instantaneous and violent.

Yes, of course. He bore the standard of that ineradicable and indomitable idea. An English writer, the author of *that book*, the spectre of Alexander Wolf, the rider atop the white horse of the Apocalypse, the man lying there on the road after I shot him—this man was a murderer. Perhaps he had no desire to be one; he seemed much too clever and cultured for that. However, it seemed impossible for him not to be familiar with the impersonal lure of murder, which I too knew so vaguely and theoretically: the lure that set the history of the world in motion that day when Cain killed his brother. That was why my imagination had returned so persistently to him all these years. His memory had always been linked so closely to the idea of murder. The idea itself was all the more tragic precisely because it was inescapable, being vested in the form of a double inevitability: carry death with you or move towards it, kill or be killed. There was no other means of stopping this blind action that Alexander Wolf personified. It was one of the thorniest concepts, simultaneously containing both the question and the answer: people have forever answered killing with killing, be it in a war or at trial, a conflict of emotions or one of interests, retribution or justice, attack or defence.

Where exactly did the allure of this type of crime lie, irrespective of how it could be interpreted or which external factors or motives brought it about? Those few seconds it takes to terminate a person's life comprise the idea of an incredible, almost superhuman, power. If under a microscope every drop of water is a whole world, then every human life must contain an enormous universe within the bounds of its transient, arbitrary casing. Even if one rejects these exaggerated—as if under a microscope—impressions, yet other evidence still remains. Every human life is connected to other human lives, those in turn are connected with others, and when we reach the logical end of this sequence of inter-relations, we approach the sum total of people inhabiting the vast surface of the terrestrial globe. The constant threat of death in all its endless diversity hangs over every man, every life: catastrophe, train crash, earthquake, tempest, war, illness, accident, all manifestations of a blind and merciless power, a peculiarity of which consists in our inability ever to predict the moment when it—this instantaneous break in the history of the world—will happen. "For ye know neither the day nor the hour..." And so, to him among us who has sufficient strength of mind to overcome a terrible resistance to this is given the opportunity to become, for some short space of time, more powerful than fate and chance, earthquake and tempest, and to know the exact moment when he'll put a stop to that long and complex evolution of thoughts, sensations and lives, the movement of life in all its variety of forms, which otherwise would have crushed him in its relentless march forward. Love, hatred, fear, regret, remorse, will, passion—any feeling and any aggregate of feelings, any law and any aggregate of laws—all is help-less before the momentary power of murder. This power belongs to me, and I, too, can become its victim. Having experienced its lure, all that remains beyond its limits seems spectral, immaterial and unimportant to me; even now, I cannot share any interest in the multitude of trivialities that constitutes the purpose of life for so many millions of people. From the moment I experience it, the world will become alien to me and I shan't be able live as they do—the others who lack this power, this understanding, this awareness of the strange fragility of everything, and even this constant, icy proximity to death.

It was the simple, logical conclusion to that distinctive philosophy, extracts of which Wolf had laid out to me. It was also a manifestation of that same notion of fixity, for me completely inadmissible, but which one could fight only with its own weapons; the use of this means of fight-ing involuntarily drew me closer to a sinister, dead world whose spectre had haunted me for so long. What else could oppose this philosophy, and why did every one of its words invariably incite an internal protest within me? I, too, understood and sensed the fragility of the so-called positive concepts, and I knew the meaning of death, but I felt neither its pull nor any fear of it. Something I couldn't quite put my finger on held me back in this painful area of understanding the final truths. I thought about it so intently that I even began to think I knew the answer to this and had known it all along, that the answer was so natural and obvious that I could never have any last-minute doubts as to how exactly it ought to go. But now, today, at this very moment, I couldn't find it.

I took out a cigarette and struck a match, which sparked and instantly went out, leaving behind the smell of half-burnt phosphorus. Then, plainly before me, I saw the dense trees of a garden in the moon's copper light, and the grey hair of my schoolteacher who was sitting next to me on a curved wooden bench. It was early autumn. At night. My final exams were to commence the following morning. I'd been working the whole evening, and so I went out into the garden. As I walked along a lengthy school corridor, my classmates told me that an hour earlier one of our teachers, a young woman of twenty-four, had taken her own life. In the garden I saw another teacher sitting on a little bench. I sat down next to him, took out a cigarette and lit a match; then, as now, it immediately went out, and I noticed that same odour.

I asked him what he made of the death of this woman and of the cruel injustice of her fate—if one may ascribe such hackneyed words as "cruel", "sad" and "undeserved" to concepts like death and fate. He was a tremendously intelligent man, perhaps the most intelligent of anyone I ever knew, and he was a brilliant conversationalist. Even those who were shy or embittered placed an unusual amount of confidence in him. He never abused, even in the slightest degree, his enormous mental and cultural superiority over others, and so talking with him was always easy.

Among other things that evening, he said to me:

"There is, of course, no single commandment whose equity can be proven beyond all doubt, just as there is no moral law that is binding without exception. Ethics exist only in as much as we are prepared to accept them. You're asking me about death. I'd say, about death and its innumerable manifestations. I perceive death and life conditionally, as two opposing origins encompassing almost everything we see, feel and comprehend. You must understand that the Law of Contrast is something like a categorical imperative: it's almost impossible for us to think beyond generalizations and contrasts."

This was so unlike anything he would tell us in the classroom. I was listening intently, trying to take in his every word.

"I'm tired," he said, "and must go to bed. Have you studied for the exam? How I'd like to be in your shoes."

He stood up. I, too, got up from the little bench. The leaves were still; a silence hung in the garden.

"There's a wonderful line in Dickens somewhere," he said. "It's worth your while remembering it. I don't recall exactly how it goes, but its meaning is this: we are given life with the vital stipulation that we bravely defend it to the last breath. Good night."

So I, too, now got up from my armchair, just as I had done from the bench where I'd been sitting with him that night, and I repeated these words that sounded somehow particularly significant then:

"We are given life with the vital stipulation that we bravely defend it to the last breath."

At that moment, the telephone began to ring. I picked up the receiver. Yelena Nikolayevna's voice asked:

"Where have you been? I've missed you. What are you doing right now?"

Hearing those first sounds of her voice, distorted as usual by the telephone, I immediately forgot everything I'd only just been thinking about; it was so total and instantaneous, as though the thoughts had never even existed.

"I'm getting up from my armchair," I said. "In my left hand I'm holding the receiver. With my right, I'm placing some cigarettes and matches into my coat pocket. Now I'm looking at the clock: it's five minutes to six. I'll be with you at a quarter past."

We dined early, at around seven o'clock. She wore a light summer dress, and we took tea in her room along with an unusually delicious chocolate cake that Annie had baked; it crumbled and melted in the mouth, and there was a lovely, subtle hint of spice in it.

"How do you find the cake?"

"Excellent," I said. "There is, however, something Negro about it, but pleasantly so. Like the far-off echo of their singing."

"You lapse into lyricism in the most particular of circumstances."

"Am I to know which?"

"Oh, it's very simple. There are two things to which you're never indifferent: food and women."

"Thank you for the flattering opinion. Might I express, in that case, my sympathy with regards to your selection?"

"I didn't say that I found these features off-putting."

I was intoxicated by her presence; this was probably evident in my eyes, as she remarked to me:

"How impatient you are, how keen! Must you hold me like that, taking my body in your arms and crushing my ribs?"

"When I'm sixty, Lenochka, I'll think on the vanity of all earthly things and the infidelity of emotions. Sometimes I think about it even now."

"Probably only in the absence of those circumstances that arouse your bent towards lyricism."

I now noticed a new trait in her, one that hadn't been there at the beginning of our intimacy: she would frequently tease me, but always in a friendly manner and without any intent of saying something truly unpleasant. Perhaps it came about because she'd been infected by my cynical attitude towards a great many things, and now she was involuntarily adopting my tone. At any rate, it seemed beyond doubt that she was acquiring, little by little, the mental freedom and spontaneity whose absence had been so conspicuous before.

I proposed getting out of town for a few days; she immediately agreed. The following morning we drove out of Paris, and, without any fixed destination in mind, we travelled around over the course of an entire week, staying within a hundred-and-fifty-kilometre radius of the city. One day, after we unexpectedly ran out of petrol, we were forced to spend a night in the forest, inside the car. There was a thunderstorm and a heavy downpour, and in the flashes of lightning I could see through the vehicle's streaming windows the trees surrounding us on all sides. Yelena Nikolayevna slept huddled up in the seat, with her warm, heavy head resting in my lap. I sat there, smoking. Whenever I lowered the window for a moment to flick the ash off my cigarette, the intense patter of raindrops falling on leaves would bore into my ears; there was a smell of earth and damp tree trunks. Somewhere, not too far off, twigs would snap with a wet crack. The rain would abate for a minute, but there would be a flash of lightning, a rumble of thunder and then torrents of water once more would begin to beat down onto the roof of the car with all their former force. I was afraid to move, lest I wake up Yelena Nikolayevna. I could scarcely keep my eyes open. My head fell back. While drifting in and out of sleep, I thought of a great many things, but first and foremost of how, no matter how complicated my life may become or whatever may befall me in the future, I would always remember that night, this woman's head in my lap, the rain and the state of drowsy happiness I found myself in. It was an old habit of mine to withhold my feelings and attempt to understand them, and so I kept seeking out the reasons for the deep-rooted, blind knowledge that one day I would experience this happiness and that there wouldn't even be anything unexpected about it, as though it were a rightful, natural thing, for which I was always destined. Right then, I was struck by the thought that if I wanted to comprehend all this and discover in some far-off place the imaginary moment from which all this began, if I wanted to explain fully why this had happened, how it had been possible and how I now came to find myself in the forest on a summer's night, in the rain, with a woman of whose existence I had known nothing only a few months before (and yet without whom I was now unable to imagine my life), I would have to spend years labouring and taxing my memory. I would probably be able to write a few volumes on it into the bargain. How was it all possible, the steady rhythm of the rain, the feeling of this head resting in my lap—my muscles had already begun to get used to the imprint made by this round, tender weight on them—this face I was looking at in the darkness, as if leaning over my own fate, and this unforgettable feeling of blissful plenitude? Throughout my life I'd seen much that was tragic or detestable; so often had I witnessed deceit, cowardice, desertion, avarice, crime and stupidity, and I was so poisoned by all this that I seemed incapable of feeling anything bearing even a distant echo of fleeting perfection. During these times, I was far removed from the doubts that usually hounded me, far from the constant feeling of sadness, far from mockery—in

brief, far from what constituted the substance of my enduring attitude towards everything that happened to me. Were
it not for what was going on right now, I thought my life
would have been lived in vain and that it would for ever
have been so, regardless of what was to come.

Never before had I felt this with such clarity as I did on
that night; I was aware that not once in my life had there
been such a particular purity of feeling. Throughout this
period, everything had been concentrated on one single
idea, and although it encompassed everything I knew and
thought, and everything that preceded this point in time, it
did contain the element of fixity that Wolf had mentioned.
Perhaps he was right, after all: if we didn't know death,
neither would we know happiness. Without knowledge of
death, we would be unable to appreciate the true value of
our finest feelings, we would be unable to know that some
of them are never to be repeated and that we can only
understand them in all their richness at the moment they
occur. Until that point we aren't destined to do so, and
afterwards it's too late.

This was one of the reasons in particular that compelled
me not to tell Yelena Nikolayevna the story about Wolf. I
had no intention at all of hiding it from her; on the contrary, I often thought of how I should be the one to tell it.
At the time, however, I was loath to let something foreign
and hostile enter the world in which we lived. I supposed
Yelena Nikolayevna to be of the same mind, as over the
course of the entire week she never once referred to the
"meeting with a spectre" that I had mentioned.

Numerous times the thought struck me that if I were to commit to paper all the conversations I had with Yelena Nikolayevna over the course of that week it would produce the most incomprehensible rubbish, offensive for its sheer lack of substance. The conversations provided an accompaniment to the play of feelings that epitomized the period, beyond which nothing else existed for us; all our surroundings seemed funny and amusing—wallpaper patterns in the hotels we stayed in, the faces of the maids or proprietresses, the menus, the outfits of the people sitting at our table, or the entirely insignificant things they occupied themselves with—because we, and no one else, were the only people to know which things bore any real significance.

We returned to Paris a week later. Urgent work awaited me, in which Yelena Nikolayevna, as ever, took an active role. The first day passed as usual. However, when she woke me the following morning I was struck by the look of alarm that flashed a few times in her eyes. Later, something transpired that had never happened before: she gave me an answer that was completely extraneous.

"What's the matter with you?"

"Nothing," she replied. "Perhaps it's silly, but I wanted to ask you something."

"Yes?"

"Do you really love me?"

"I suppose so."

"That's all I wanted to know."

"How old are you?"

"No, really, it's important to know."

We parted as usual, late at night; she complained of being tired and said that she wouldn't come until four o'clock the following afternoon.

"Fine," I said. "A rest would do you good."

I immediately fell into a deep sleep, but I awoke soon after. Then I dozed off, and after an hour I opened my eyes again. I couldn't understand what was wrong with me; I even wondered whether I might have been poisoned by something. I was in a state of anxiety, all the more incomprehensible as there really didn't seem to be any grounds for it at all. Sleep finally deserted me, and I got up sometime after five o'clock in the morning. Nothing like this had happened to me in years.

Convinced that I wouldn't get back to sleep, I drank a cup of black coffee, took a bath and began to shave. My face stared out at me from the mirror, and although I saw it every morning of my life I could never quite accustom myself to its severe ugliness, much as I couldn't get used to the wild, foreign look in my eyes. When I thought of myself, of the feelings I had, of the things I thought I understood so well, I imagined myself somehow abstractly, because that other visual recollection was painful and unpleasant for me. No sooner would I call to mind my physical appearance than the finest, most lyrical, wonderful visions would vanish in an instant—so monstrous was its disparity with the intangible, glittering world that existed in my imagination. It seemed to me that there could be no greater contrast than that between my inner life and my outward appearance; sometimes I even imagined that I was trapped in someone else's strange, almost hateful body. I calmly endured the sight of my essentially average naked body, whose muscles moved obediently and evenly, and were arranged exactly as they were supposed to be. It was a commonplace, inexpressive body, not overly thin, though devoid of any excess fat. Where the face began, however, it transformed into something so contrary to what ought to have been there that I would always avert the gaze of those foreign eyes and try not to think about it. Thus now, after a sleepless night, this unpleasant feeling was much more intense than usual.

I had only just finished dressing and was intending to sit down to work when, suddenly, the telephone in my room began to ring. I looked at the clock in astonishment; it was twenty minutes to six. I had no idea who could be calling so early. After some hesitation I picked up the receiver. A drunken voice, in which I did, however, detect some familiar intonations, said:

"Good morning, dearest."

"What's all this?"

"Don't you recognize me?"

It was a man pretending to be a woman. I recognized the voice; it belonged to a fellow journalist, a rather amiable if wayward man. He would periodically drink himself to the point of stupefaction, and this in most cases would be accompanied by some fantastic exploits: he would resolve to pay a night-time visit to some senator who had allegedly invited him a few days previously, or else he would set out for place de la Bourse to send a telegram to his aunt who lived in Lyons, informing her that he was quite well "despite all the rumours being spread about him".

"As you'll no doubt have guessed," he continued more or less coherently, "I met a friend who invited me… Odette, stop harassing me. I'm quite sober."

Odette was his wife, a very sensible, level-headed woman. A second later I heard her voice (she had evidently taken the receiver from him).

"Hello," she said. "This drunken idiot was calling you to discuss some business."

"Tell him it's top-drawer stuff," a voice said in the background.

"It's just that your protégé Curly Pierrot is about to be arrested. Philippe blabbed everything under interrogation. André"—this was her husband—"is too drunk to be able to do anything. The material for the article really is top-drawer. I know you're no fan of gangster stories and melodramas; you think they're bad stuff, don't you? I wouldn't have disturbed you, only it's about our good friend. Go and see Jean; I'd take a revolver if I were you. Just in case."

"Thanks, Odette," I said. "I owe you for this. I'm on my way."

"All right," she replied, and rang off.

Jean, the man whom I was supposed to be meeting, was a police inspector; I'd known him for a long time and we were on friendly terms. He had a great gift for reincarnation, or, more likely, was the victim of some peculiar case of split personality. In carrying out his professional duties, for example interrogating any run-of-the-mill suspect, he would always wear his cap tilted back, keep a cigarette in the corner of his mouth, and speak curtly, monosyllabically and almost exclusively in argot. However, as soon as he began addressing an investigator or a journalist, he would transform instantaneously and become a man of high pretensions: "If you would be so kind as to take the trouble to analyse some of the facts as a preliminary, so to speak…" One had to suppose that it was he who had interrogated Philippe, Curly Pierrot's right-hand man. By all accounts, a police car would shortly be leaving for Sèvres, where Pierrot was in hiding, and this time he had little chance of escape. I hesitated for a moment, then picked up the receiver and dialled. I remembered that the telephone was located next to Pierrot's bed. Presently, an exasperated female voice asked:

"What's wrong?"

"Get Pierrot," I replied. "Tell him there's a call from rue la Fayette."

This was a code name.

"He isn't here, he hasn't come back yet. And Philippe's been missing for two days. I don't know what to think."

"Philippe's given the game away," I said. "Try to find Pierrot at all costs, wherever he is, and warn him. Tell him not to come home. In an hour it'll be too late."

I hung up, took the revolver out of my writing desk, checked that it was loaded, put it in my coat pocket and left the building. Then I took a taxi to Jean's.

All this distracted me from the mental anxiety I'd been

feeling; sitting in the car, I now gave some thought to the fate of Curly Pierrot, "*Pierrot le frisé*", whom I knew so well and pitied so much, although perhaps by the standards of classical justice he didn't merit any pity at all: he was a professional looter with several lives on his conscience. I met him around six years ago, after he shot dead his first victim, an ex-boxer by the name of Albert. By pure chance—it was four o'clock in the morning—I wound up in the café that housed his secret headquarters, although I hadn't the slightest idea of this at the time. I sat down at a table and began to write. There were some drunkards shouting and arguing at the bar, when a deathly silence suddenly descended. With uncommon expressiveness and what was an unexpectedly humane tone after all these howling voices, someone (I had no idea who he was back then) said:

"Do you want what happened to Albert to happen to you?"

There was no answer. I carried on writing, keeping my head down. The café emptied.

"Well, I've scared them off," said the same voice, "but who's that one over there?"

He was talking about me.

"I don't know," replied the owner. "This is the first time I've seen him."

I could hear footsteps approaching my table. I raised my eyes and saw a man of average height, very solidly built, with a clean-shaven, solemn face; he was wearing a light-grey suit, a navy-blue shirt and a canary-yellow tie. I was struck by the plaintive look in his eyes, evidently accounted for by the fact that he was drunk. He met my gaze and asked without any lead-up:

"What are you doing here?"

"Writing."

"And? What are you writing?"

"An article."

"An article?"

"Yes."

This seemed to surprise him.

"So you aren't from the police?"

"No, I'm a journalist."

"Do you know who I am?"

"No."

"They call me Curly Pierrot."

Then I remembered that a few days previously there had been articles in two newspapers about the death of a boxer called Albert, who had stood trial fourteen times and had been incarcerated in a variety of prisons. The headlines read: "Gangsters at War" and "Boxer Murdered in Revenge Attack". There had also been mention of some woman who was the alleged cause of all this. "The police have little doubt that the perpetrator of the crime is Pierre Dieudonné, alias 'Curly Pierrot', who is wanted urgently by the authorities. According to latest reports, he has managed to leave Paris and is located, most probably, on the Riviera."

Yet here that same Pierrot was standing in front of me, in a café on boulevard Saint-Denis.

"So you haven't gone to the Riviera?"

"No."

He sat down opposite me and began to think. After a few minutes he asked:

"What actually do you write about?"

"About whatever I have to, about a lot of things."

"But you don't write novels?"

"I haven't written one yet, but maybe I'll write one someday. Why do you ask?"

We talked as though we were old acquaintances. He enquired after my name and which newspapers I worked for; he said he could tell me a lot of intriguing stories, given the occasion, and invited me to drop by the café sometime. Then he and I parted.

We met many times after that, and indeed he did tell me some interesting anecdotes. Thanks to his candour, I often had at my disposal certain information that the police lacked, since he was so exceptionally well informed in this particular area. He was without doubt an outstanding man; he had a natural intelligence, and by this he distinguished himself sharply from his "colleagues", who mostly stood out just as much for their unquestionable stupidity. Like most men in his trade, he gambled recklessly at the races and was a daily reader of the newspaper *Veine*; that aside, however, he did occasionally read books, and in particular novels by Dekobra, which he liked very much.

"That's how it's done!" he would say to me. "Eh? What do you think?"

I always imagined that he would meet a bad end one day, not only because his profession was a dangerous one, but also for another reason: he was forever attracted to forbidden fruits, and yet he understood the difference between his life's pursuits and the pursuits of others—people who were infinitely far beyond his reach.

One day he showed up in a red Bugatti. He was wearing a new fawn suit with his beloved canary tie, the customary rings glittering on his fingers.

"What do you think?" he asked me. "Could I go to a reception at the embassy like this, just like those guys they write about in the papers? Eh? 'We noted…'"

I shook my head. This surprised him.

"You think I'm badly dressed?"

"Yes."

"Me? Do you know how much I paid for this suit?"

"No, but that's beside the point."

I would never have suspected my negative appraisal of his mode of dress capable of causing him so much disappointment. He took a seat opposite me and said:

"Tell me, then, why you think I'm inappropriately dressed."

I explained to him as best I could. He looked puzzled. I added:

"Anyway, it'd be easy to single you out just by looking at those clothes. Anyone with a certain understanding, shall we say, wouldn't need to recognize you or ask for your papers. He'd know the sort of man he's dealing with just by the suit, the tie and the rings."

"What about the car?"

"It's a racing car. What's the use of it in a city? In any case, they're a rarity. Take an average dark-coloured car; no one will notice it."

He sat in silence, propping his head up with his hand.

"What's the matter?"

"I'm at sixes and sevens when you talk like that," he said. "I'm beginning to understand what I shouldn't. You tell me the books I like are bad. You know more about this than I do. I can't talk to you as an equal because I don't have the education. I'm a low-down guy, *je suis un inférieur*, that's what's the matter. Besides, I'm a gangster. And other people are just better than me."

I shrugged my shoulders. He looked at me intently and asked:

"Tell me frankly: do you agree with me?"

"No," I said.

"Why?"

"Yes, you're a gangster," I said. "You don't dress as you ought to, and you don't have a certain education. That's quite true. But if you think that any big name you read about in the papers—a banker, a minister, a senator—is your better, then you're wrong. He works and, more importantly, takes fewer risks. He's addressed as 'Chairman' or 'Minister'. He dresses differently, and better, and indeed he does have a certain education, although that's far from always the case. But as a man he's no better than you, so you needn't worry. I don't know whether this will console you, but it's my opinion nonetheless."

Pierrot had a great weakness for the fairer sex, and the majority of the "scores" he had to settle—those which ended so tragically—came about namely as a result of these women.

"They'll be the end of you one day—*peut-être bien, tu mourras par les femmes*," I said to him. "What's more, it'll be down to the ones who aren't worth the trouble in the first place."

It wasn't difficult to predict. Even now, as I approached Jean's office in the taxi, it was on account of a woman that Pierrot's hideout had been let slip to those from whom he needed to conceal it most of all.

The position was hopeless. His activities had become particularly violent of late; robbery followed robbery, and the police were finally cracking down on all those from whom they could expect some assistance in the matter. The woman who had caused all this was the wife of Pierrot's deputy, Philippe. Philippe was an enormous man, a Hercules, fearing, in his own words, nothing and no one on earth, apart from his boss, who was renowned for being a superb shot.

I had seen this woman a number of times; she had recently become Pierrot's lover, and I'm of the belief that it was precisely for this reason that Inspector Jean managed to obtain a confession from Philippe. With the same inalterable poor taste that distinguished her whole milieu, she was given the nickname "the Panther". She had enormous, wild, dark-blue eyes behind eyelashes that were painted a similar shade, her hair was black with tight curls and never had to be styled, she had a large mouth with impressive, heavily painted lips, her bust was small and her body lithe; never did I see a more ferocious creature. She bit her lovers until she drew blood, she screeched and clawed, and no one recalled ever hearing her speak with a calm voice. Around three weeks previously, she left Philippe; it was she who answered the telephone when I rang through to Sèvres before going to Inspector Jean's.

When I entered, Inspector Jean was sitting on a chair with his cap tilted back. Opposite him, with his elbows on his knees, sat Philippe, in handcuffs. He had a pallid, dirty face, which bore the traces of dried rivulets of perspiration. He was very dirty and smelt strongly of sweat; the atmosphere in the room was hot and stifling. Jean said to him:

"That'll do for now. You did well to be honest. If you'd kept quiet, I'd have easily had your hide. Now you'll do some time inside and that'll be the end of it. It's nothing to a man of your health."

I looked at Philippe; he lowered his eyes. Two policemen led him away.

"I suppose," said Jean, turning to me, "and flatter myself with the hope that you'll share my supposition… I suppose that Pierrot is sleeping the sleep of the righteous at present. My, how many of today's phrases are so relative! Our mutual friends called to say that you want to come with us. Do I understand correctly?"

"Yes," I said. "I have a taxi waiting."

"We'll leave in five minutes."

It was around seven o'clock in the morning when the police car stopped a few metres from the small villa that Pierrot lived in. The shutters were closed. The morning sun, already warm, lit up the narrow street. It was so quiet at this early hour.

I stopped the taxi behind the police car and got out,

slamming the door behind me. A heavy, languid weariness gripped me. I imagined Pierrot alone (because, of course, he couldn't count on the help of his lover) in this dark, closed-up house that he was trapped in. Of course, it might have been possible to jump out of the low side window into the little garden adjoining the house, but there were policemen stationed along the railings. There was no hope of escape under these circumstances.

There were six policemen in total. Each of their faces was inscribed with the same mixed expression of gloom and loathing. I'm sure that my face bore exactly the same expression.

One of the policemen knocked at the door and shouted for Pierrot to open up.

"Step aside," said Jean. "He might shoot."

But there was no shot. I began to hope that maybe they had managed to warn Pierrot. Following the inspector's words, a tense silence descended; from the outside, they could feel the presence of a man with a revolver, lurking inside the dark house. Each of the policemen was familiar with his reputation as a marksman.

"Pierrot," said Jean, "I advise you to give yourself up. You'll save us a difficult job. You know you can't escape."

There was no reply. Another minute of agonizing silence passed.

"I repeat, Pierrot," said Jean, "give yourself up."

Then a voice cut through the silence; the initial sound of it sent a shiver down my spine. It was undoubtedly Pierrot's incomprehensibly calm, humane voice, which I knew so well and which now seemed so particularly terrible, because in a few minutes, lest there be some miracle, it would fall silent for ever. The fact that the energy of a young and healthy man could be heard in this voice was unbearably painful.

"What difference does it make?" he said. "If I give myself up, I'll be for the guillotine. I don't want to die that way, *je voudrais mourir autrement.*"

What came next happened with incredible speed. I heard the snap of branches in the garden, then a shot was fired, and one of the policemen standing by the railings slumped to the ground. I saw Pierrot scramble up the railings—he was hindered by the revolver he was carrying in his hand—then he jumped down into the street, and that very second shots began to ring out from all sides. Apart from the policeman who had been killed, no one else was wounded, which seemed utterly astonishing. They all threw themselves at the spot where Pierrot had fallen. Later I realized why not a single one of them had been injured: the very first bullet had hit Pierrot in the hand he was using to hold the revolver, smashing his fingers. He was lying literally in a pool of blood: I never knew that there was so much blood in the human body. I went up to Pierrot. There was a gurgling noise coming from either his throat or his lungs. Then the gurgling stopped. Pierrot's eyes met mine, and he wheezed:

"Thank you. It was too late."

I cannot comprehend how he found the strength to utter those words. I stood motionless and heard my teeth chattering from a feeling of helpless agitation, anger and an intolerable inner chill.

"You warned him?" Jean asked me.

I remained silent for a few seconds. Pierrot made one last spasm and died. Then I said:

"I think he was delirious."

Pierrot's body was taken away. The policemen left. Two men in workmen's clothing came with a wheelbarrow full of sand and scattered it over the pool of blood in the road. The sun already stood high in the sky. I paid the taxi driver and departed on foot, heading back towards Paris.

The feeling of nausea and dull sorrow was unrelenting; periodically I'd experience chills, even though it was quite a warm day. An article about Pierrot was to appear in the newspaper the following morning. "Tragic End to Curly Pierrot". I imagined the editor and his perpetually excited face, and again I could hear his hoarse, desperate voice: "Half the success is in getting the headline right; it hooks the reader in. Then it's your job to keep him with you until the very end. Nothing too literary. Got it?" In the beginning, when I hardly knew him and depended on him, I would just shrug my shoulders in vexation. Later on I realized that he was right in his own way, and that attempts at great literature were quite out of place in newspaper articles.

As was my habit, I went into the first comparatively pleasant-looking café I came across, asked for a coffee and some paper, and, chain-smoking, set to work on the article about Pierrot. Naturally, I was unable to write it as I would have liked to write it, or say in it what I would have liked to say. Instead, however, I gave a detailed account of a sunny morning in a peaceful suburb of Paris, of the villas on the quiet streets, and of this unexpected drama that was to be the culmination of Pierrot's tempestuous life. I couldn't resist dedicating a few lines to the Panther, the very thought of whom provoked nothing but loathing in me. I wrote about Philippe, about the bar on boulevard Saint-Denis, and about Pierrot's life story, which he had told me, interjecting every minute: "Just imagine!"

Later, I found a telephone box and called Inspector Jean: "Any news?"

"Nothing special. Although the Panther assures me that early this morning someone made a telephone call to her, insisting that she warn Pierrot."

"Well, why didn't she do it?"

"She claims that Pierrot got back only a minute before we showed up."

"That seems unlikely to me; it's too much of a coincidence. I don't even know whether it's worth mentioning in the article. Anyway, I'm giving your role in this a special mention. No, no, I couldn't let it go unnoticed."

I hung up, paused for a few moments and, overcoming my initial reluctance, added four lines about a "mysterious telephone call".

By the time I had finished the article and sent it off to the editorial office, it was already nearing midday. I felt so

ghastly; the state of depression I had been in during my
bout of insomnia the previous night had intensified so much
that I hardly noticed what was going on around me any
more. Thinking only of that distressing feeling, I automati-
cally entered an unassuming little restaurant not far from
boulevard Montmartre. Scarcely had I let the first piece
of meat pass my lips than suddenly I saw Pierrot's corpse
right before me, and just then the pungent stench of sweat
coming from Philippe at the end of his interrogation hit
my nose. It took a great effort to stay the urge to vomit. I
gulped down some water and made a swift exit, telling the
proprietress that I felt ill and had stomach cramps.

It was a hot day, and the streets were full of people. I
walked unsteadily, like a drunkard, vainly trying to shake
off this unbearable sense of weariness and an impenetrable
fog that was enshrouding my senses. As I walked, I was
unconsciously absorbing all this noise, unaware of its exact
meaning. The nausea would occasionally rise up in my
throat, and at those moments I felt that there could be
nothing more tragic than these crowds of people in the
midday sun on the boulevards of Paris. Only then did I
realize how terribly tired I was and how I had felt this way
for so long. I thought how pleasant it would be to lie down
and fall asleep, and to wake up on the other side of these
events and sensations that afforded me no rest.

Suddenly, I remembered that I was expecting Yelena
Nikolayevna at four o'clock. She was the only person I
wanted to see, and so I decided to go to her directly rather
than wait. But even as I ascended her staircase, this dull,

aching weariness refused to leave me. When at last I reached her apartment, I took out my keys and anxiously turned them in the lock. I was unable to account for this peculiar anxiety, but I understood it soon after having flung open the door: I could hear raised voices coming from Yelena Nikolayevna's room. Before I could think about what might have been the cause of this, I was seized by an inert horror. I had no time to think. Yelena Nikolayevna's desperate cry reached me; her terrible, unrecognizable voice was shouting:

"Never, do you hear? Never!"

I ran, as if in a dream, along the corridor leading to her room. In the corner I saw Annie's face, grey from fright, although I recalled this detail only later. Unconsciously, I think, I had already been holding the revolver in my hand for some time. Suddenly I heard the crash and clatter of broken glass; it was followed by a shot and a second cry that was devoid of any words, sounding more like convulsive intakes of breath: "Ah!… Ah!… Ah!…" I was already at the glass door, which was lying half-open; from the threshold I could see Yelena Nikolayevna standing by the window, and, half-turned towards her, the silhouette of a man who was also holding a revolver. Without raising my arm, almost without even taking aim (it would have been impossible to miss at that distance), I shot him twice in quick succession. He spun around, stiffened and then slumped down to the floor.

I stood motionless for a few seconds, everything spinning in a haze before me. However, I did notice blood on Yelena Nikolayevna's white dress: her left shoulder had been wounded. I learnt afterwards that, in defending herself, she had thrown a glass vase at her assailant almost at the same time as he pulled the trigger; this accounted for the deflection of his bullet.

He was lying flat out on the floor, his arms spread wide; his head had fallen next to her foot. I took a step forward and leant over him. Time suddenly seemed to start swirling and disappearing, bearing away the long years of my life in this inconceivably rapid shift.

There, staring back at me from the grey rug covering the floor of the room, were the dead eyes of Alexander Wolf.